FRANÇOISE DE GRAFFIGNY

Letters from a
Peruvian Woman

Texts and Translations
Modern Language Association of America

Carmen Chaves Tesser, chair; Eugene C. Eoyang, Michael R. Katz, Robert J. Rodini, Judith L. Ryan, Mario J. Valdés, and Renée Waldinger, series editors

Texts

1. Isabelle de Charrière, *Lettres de Mistriss Henley publiées par son amie*. Ed. Joan Hinde Stewart and Philip Stewart. 1993.
2. Françoise de Graffigny, *Lettres d'une Péruvienne*. Introd. Joan DeJean and Nancy K. Miller. 1993.

Translations

1. Isabelle de Charrière, *Letters of Mistress Henley Published by Her Friend*. Trans. Philip Stewart and Jean Vaché. 1993.
2. Françoise de Graffigny, *Letters from a Peruvian Woman*. Trans. David Kornacker. 1993.

FRANÇOISE DE GRAFFIGNY

Letters from a Peruvian Woman

Translated by David Kornacker

Introduction by
Joan DeJean and Nancy K. Miller

The Modern Language Association of America
New York 1993

Translation of the Garnier-Flammarion edition of *Lettres d'une Péru-vienne*, by Madame de Graffigny. Translated by permission of Librarie Ernest Flammarion.

© 1993 by The Modern Language Association of America
All rights reserved. Printed in the United States of America

Library of Congress Cataloging-in-Publication Data

Grafigny, Mme de (Françoise d'Issembourg d'Happoncourt), 1695–1758.
 [Lettres d'une Péruvienne. English]
 Letters from a Peruvian woman / Françoise de Graffigny ; translated by David Kornacker ; introduction by Joan DeJean and Nancy K. Miller.
 p. cm. — (Texts and translations. Translations ; 2.)
 Includes bibliographical references.
 ISBN 0-87352-778-X (paper)
 1. France—Social life and customs—18th century—Fiction.
 2. Peruvians—France—Fiction. 3. Women—France—Fiction.
 I. Title. II. Series.
 PQ1986.L4E4   1993
 843'.5—dc20   93-37517

Published by The Modern Language Association of America
10 Astor Place, New York, New York 10003-6981

Printed on recycled paper

TABLE OF CONTENTS

INTRODUCTION

No work of eighteenth-century French literature has benefited more clearly from twentieth-century American experiments in canon revision than has Françoise de Graffigny's *Letters from a Peruvian Woman* (*Lettres d'une Péruvienne*).[1] In recent years, Graffigny's tale of an Inca princess's initiation into the society, the politics, and the culture of eighteenth-century France has become a staple of reading lists in North America. Today's teachers are thereby restoring this work to its original prominence: a best-seller in its day, *Lettres d'une Péruvienne* was reprinted forty-six times in the thirty years following its initial publication in 1747.[2] However, the novel fell out of favor in the nineteenth century. Furthermore, when the French pedagogical canon was opened to eighteenth-century works, Graffigny's novel—along with the production of her female contemporaries in general—was denied classic status.

This situation would hardly have surprised Graffigny, who firmly believed that women were at a disadvantage in the literary marketplace. In her extensive correspondence, she consistently downplays her literary efforts —not an unusual stance for someone who became an author almost by accident. Born Françoise d'Issembourg d'Happoncourt in 1695, she grew up in Lorraine. A disastrous marriage in 1712 to François Huguet (the couple took the name de Graffigny from one of his family properties) ended with a legal separation, a decree that was then obtained only with great difficulty. Graffigny's was probably granted to her only because her husband, after having squandered his inheritance, had begun to dissipate her family's money as well. However, the marriage was also troubled in other ways: in unpublished testimony she prepared for the court proceedings, Graffigny cited witnesses who certified that she had been the victim of frequent and violent physical abuse at his hands. After the separation, she moved to Lunéville, where she was under the protection of the ducal court. Subsequently, Graffigny turned to literature to support herself. In 1738, at age forty-four, she took up residence in Paris, where she moved in a literary milieu. During her career, she wrote stories, notably "Nouvelle espagnole" 'Spanish Story' (1745); two plays, *Cénie* (1750), a sentimental comedy, and *La fille d'Aristide* 'Aristide's Daughter' (the first was staged at the Comédie-Française with great success; the second, when staged there in 1758, the year of Graffigny's death, was a failure); a number of fables, destined for the education of the children of the Imperial Court at Vienna; and one novel.

In many ways, her *Letters from a Peruvian Woman* respects epistolary conventions well established by the mid-eighteenth century. In Zilia's initial epistles to her beloved Aza the reader can hear echoes of Mariane, the plaintive heroine of the *Lettres portugaises* (1668; *Portuguese Letters*), the original French epistolary novel. At first Zilia, like her precursor, "writes to the moment"—as

Samuel Richardson termed one of his favorite epistolary techniques—collapsing as much as possible the distance between event and narration and suggesting thereby a present tense with an impossible plenitude. For Zilia, this plenitude is necessary to keep alive the illusion of Aza's presence in her life. "I love you, I think it, I feel it still, I say it for the last time," she writes him at the end of letter 6. This letter marks the first turning point in her correspondence. Faced with the realization that she is being taken away from her homeland, where the illusion of a dialogue with Aza can more plausibly be kept alive, Zilia contemplates suicide: nothingness is preferable to existence outside the plenitude created by writing to the moment.

But then letter 7 begins the revelation of a new Zilia. She explains that to choose suicide, in the manner of numerous abandoned women in epistolary literature (notably several heroines of Ovid's *Epistulae heroidum* 'Letters from Heroines,' one of the most prominent models for Graffigny's age) or in the manner of Montesquieu's Roxane (of his *Persian Letters*), is merely to elect "weakness as the principle behind our heroism." Graffigny creates a radically new type of epistolary heroine, a model for the age of Enlightenment. The new type of "heroinism" (to borrow the term coined by Ellen Moers) she proposes through Zilia is both far more active and far more overtly philosophic.

In letter 9, Zilia learns that she is in the hands of the French, who are bringing her to their homeland. She also announces to Aza, "I seek enlightenment [lumières] with an urgency that consumes me." This appearance of "lumières," the code word for subversive eighteenth-century philosophic activity, announces the major change in Graffigny's heroine that occurs when she arrives on French soil. Timidly at first, but with ever greater force as Zilia's knowledge of the French and their language increases, Graffigny uses her heroine as a voice of social satire. In letter 18, Zilia, who initially communicates with Aza in her native "language," by quipus, or knotted weavings, describes the process by which she learns to write— and to write in French. After her initiation into the art of writing, she says that she is "restored to [her]self." Zilia is beginning to realize, as did the heroine of the *Lettres portugaises* before her, that, from this point on, she will be writing not only for the beloved who never answers her letters but also for herself. Once she has been "restored to herself," Zilia begins her critique of French society.

Before the novel ends, Zilia becomes a far bolder practitioner of this dominant Enlightenment discourse than are the heroes created by any of Graffigny's male contemporaries. She forces readers to confront such controversial issues as the cult of the superfluous in France (letter 28); the lack of self-respect ("le respect pour soi-même") that she feels is widespread in France (letter 34); and the corruption of aristocratic values, caused, she believes, by that century's equivalent of our century's culture of narcissism (letter 29).

Graffigny even uses Zilia to voice some of the most vehement feminist protest in eighteenth-century literature.[3] She blames the "scornful" attitude of the French toward women on the superficiality of women's education —which typically took place in convent schools. Graffigny reserves her most outspoken criticism for marriage as it was then institutionalized among French aristocrats. Women became brides when they were too young and were ill-prepared for their new life. Instead of attempting to compensate for this lack of early education, husbands gave their wives a freedom so unstructured and unsupervised that it was dangerous to those untrained to deal with it. Allowed absolute authority over their wives, husbands could punish severely even "the appearance of a slight infidelity," whereas wives, even if they were abused and reduced to "indigence" by a husband's extravagance, had no protection under the law: "it seems that in France the bonds of marriage are reciprocal only at the moment the wedding is celebrated and that thereafter only wives must be subject to them" (letter 34).

This unflinching critique best illustrates the radical nature of Zilia's evolution. By the end of Graffigny's novel, the Inca princess originally quite ignorant of life outside the Temple of the Sun has come to know a foreign culture from within. Zilia's initial loss of status when she is stripped of her rank as a result of the Spanish conquest undoubtedly explains her ability to attain a degree of insight rare among foreign characters in eighteenth-century fiction. The possession of such knowledge naturally forces Zilia to confront the thorny question of her ultimate place in French society and to decide whether she will attempt to live, not only in French and among the French, but as though she were native born. Well before Zilia can formulate her boldest social protest, she realizes that she fits into no category in the French social hierarchy —what the following century would begin to call its class system (and Graffigny's vocabulary here may be the earliest use of "classe" in its modern meaning): "I have neither gold nor land nor an occupation, yet I must be one of the citizens of this city. Oh heavens above, to what class

am I to assign myself?" (letter 21). By the time Graffigny
uses her as a mouthpiece to vindicate the rights of women
in letter 34, Zilia is ready to take her place among "the
citizens of the city." Graffigny's response to the dilemma
Zilia poses with regard to the "class" of the foreign women
offers what may seem a decidedly utopian solution to the
problems of multiculturalism. It can also be seen as an
indication of the place Graffigny reserved for her novel in
the French tradition.

Zilia's assimilation officially begins as soon as she deliv-
ers her attack on marriage. At first, the process is con-
trolled by Déterville, the French suitor who has supervised
her life ever since his fellow countrymen captured her
along with the Spanish ship on which she was taken from
Peru. Déterville "transforms" Inca gold, notably the gold
throne from which Aza had been destined to rule over
his people, into a small estate and a chest of French gold
coins. The relics of Zilia's native culture thus secure her
class status in France. At this point, Déterville fully
expects that Zilia will want to complete her initiation into
Frenchness by accepting his proposal of marriage. In her
final letter, however, Zilia asks him to forget marriage and
all "tumultuous feelings" and to be content instead with
friendship (letter 41). Her decision, which continues to
frustrate readers today, drove their eighteenth-century
counterparts to a veritable frenzy of disappointment.
Graffigny received numerous letters from readers who
begged her to change the novel's ending and give them
the marriage they clearly felt they had been led to expect.
Graffigny remained obstinate in her refusal.

She could hardly have reversed a decision so fundamen-
tal to her heroine's ultimate self-definition. When Zilia

first understands Déterville's intentions, she blurts out: "How could that be? . . . You are not at all of my nation" (letter 23). From the beginning, Graffigny makes it clear that Incas in general do not understand the incest taboo. Zilia's unequivocal response here, however, may indicate that she does understand a different taboo. Her use of "nation" in the sense of "people" in this context perhaps suggests that she does not believe in assimilation by what our modern vocabulary would call racial mixing. Or it may signify a rejection of the possibility of cultural assimilation. In either case, Zilia refuses to marry a Frenchman and decides to preserve instead her sense of difference by living in a way unknown to the French as she has portrayed them.

Her only true precursor is the heroine of an earlier novel, *La Princesse de Clèves* (1678). In a famously controversial ending, Lafayette offered readers a woman who, although free to remarry after her husband's death, rejects her ardent suitor in favor of life alone on an isolated estate. This French princess's decision is so laconically explained—she speaks only of her need for repose ("repos") and her sense of duty ("devoir")—that for over three centuries readers have found it open to the most diverse interpretations. Graffigny's Inca princess is more specific about the desires that are responsible for her decision to renounce marriage.

Already at the end of letter 32, well before her critique of the French has become its most passionate, Zilia introduces the rhetoric central to her final scenario for self-preservation in the midst of a world with values she cannot respect: "Fortunate is the nation having only nature for its guide, truth for its principle, and virtue as its driving force." Nature, truth, and virtue—Zilia's trinity of public values announces the private values she defines for Déterville at the novel's close, the values she feels would be threatened, were she to marry him: "The pleasure of being . . . that happiness so pure, 'I am, I live, I exist,' could bring happiness all by itself . . . if one treasured it as befits its worth."

When her heroine thus prefers self-knowledge and self-possession to passionate romantic love, Graffigny harks back to Lafayette's novel, the greatest work of seventeenth-century French prose fiction. Unlike the Princess of Clèves, however, about whom the reader knows only that her life after the novel's end was "rather short," Zilia has a precise occupation. Inside the "château of her own," she becomes a writer, translating her first letters into French. At the same time, Graffigny's novel is a precursor of the work lit-erary history (the same literary history that refused *Letters from a Peruvian Woman* a place in the eighteenth-century canon) has pronounced the greatest French novel of the eighteenth century, Rousseau's *Julie, ou la Nouvelle Héloïse* 'Julie, or the New Eloise' (1761). Zilia's evolution takes her from her initial rhetoric of pure sentimentality to her final voice—the expression of pure being, that is, exis-tence in which the self is at one with nature. With Zilia's ultimate rhetorical stance, Graffigny announces, long before Rousseau, the Romantic tradition in French litera-ture. In addition, the type of relation Zilia offers Déter-ville foreshadows that on which Rousseau's lovers, Julie and Saint-Preux, eventually agree (and which they never successfully negotiate).

Letters from a Peruvian Woman can be seen as an essen-tial link in the early development of the novel in France.

Since its appearance on the pedagogical scene, the landscape of eighteenth-century literature has taken on excit-
ing new contours.

Joan DeJean

The publisher's preface to *Letters from a Peruvian Woman*
situates Graffigny's novel within the great anthropological project of the Enlightenment: the interrogation of
what we today like to call Eurocentrism. Although in the
process the writers and philosophers of eighteenth-century France necessarily found themselves caught up in the
seductions of the exotic other, it's still important to see
how as critics they brought self-consciousness to bear on
the gaze of cultural domination. "Comment," Montesquieu famously asked in his *Lettres persanes (Persian Letters)*, "peut-on être Persan?" 'How can one be Persian?'
Who defines what otherness is? What does our imagination of another subjectivity tell us about the limits of our
own? What, for instance, does it mean to be French?

Through the fiction of the editorial frame, Graffigny
gets to ask these questions again herself, but with a difference. Graffigny's Zilia, ethnographer-heroine, is dou-
bly other: she is Peruvian *and* female. "How can one be
Peruvian?" What does it mean to be woman and other
in France? The mark of gender in the designation of
nationality works in several ways: it situates Graffigny's
story in relation to Montesquieu's; it raises the possibility
of a feminist critique of Enlightenment strategies; it figures the position of the woman novelist and her relation
to the prestige of philosophical discourses, and in particular to the *roman philosophique* 'philosophical novel.'

Graffigny's title also performs another important displacement: the move from the adjective—*persanes*—to the noun—*Péruvienne*—emphasizes the identity of the letter writer, her singular subjectivity over the national "origin" of her correspondence.

In the 1752 edition of the novel we are using here, a "Historical Introduction" follows the prefatory note and rehearses in poignant brevity the history of suffering of the Peruvian people at the hands of Spanish colonizers in the sixteenth century.[4] Graffigny takes this opportunity to enlist in her ethnographic undertaking the essay "On Coaches," in which Montaigne reflects on the relativity and fragility of human knowledge, especially the knowledge of cultures not one's own. She quotes him to support her account of imperialism and perhaps to align her work with the literary authority of an older tradition of social commentary in France as well. This thumbnail introduction also allows Graffigny to identify the sources of her anthropological knowledge: El Inca Garcilaso de la Vega's book on the Incas, a popular history translated from Spanish into French in 1633 and reprinted most recently in 1744. Montaigne's contemporary, he seems to be Graffigny's primary source for information about the Incas; his *Royal Commentaries of the Incas* is still in print and part of the historical record. The cultural detail essential to Graffigny's fiction is the *quipu* (or *quipo*, as it is also spelled). Quipus were a system of knotting used throughout the Inca empire for all the record-keeping requirements of the bureaucracy; anthropologists today characterize the knots as the emblem of Inca culture. Strictly speaking, they are not a form of writing, but Graffigny, following Garcilaso, is tempted by the analogy that likens knotting to writing. The seduction of the analogy is another way of understanding the subversion of authority Graffigny's novel takes as a central theme, for—again, strictly speaking—the *quipucamayu*, the scribe of Inca chronicles and inventory, was not likely to have been a woman in love or even a woman writer.

Graffigny's appropriation of these cultural materials for her critique of eighteenth-century French society is not random. Given the great vogue of the exotic, she might have traveled to any number of places in her imagination; Voltaire and Montesquieu had pointed the way. But she chose the quipu because it allowed her to represent the stakes of women's writing—literally and metaphorically—in a way that naturalized her audacity. Just as the critics swallowed the implausibility of Zilia's rapid transfer from sixteenth-century Spain to eighteenth-century France, no one challenged her role as cultural critic and translator. Because Zilia was a victim of violence, carried off against her will to a foreign land, the daring of her self-invention —or, rather, Graffigny's originality—provided its own alibi. Zilia's vulnerability at the hands of her captors masked the less orthodox plot of self-determination implicit in her critical positioning as an outsider.

Zilia's uniqueness as a heroine has to do, as we have seen, with Graffigny's own knotting of several literary traditions: the philosophical tale, the epistolary novel, and Lafayette's legacy of heroinism. Although Graffigny does not invoke the *Lettres portugaises*, a seventeenth-century epistolary text generally thought to have launched the vogue of love-letter novels in which the heroine writes repeatedly to her lover of her love and misery, Graffigny's readers would not have missed the indirect reference.

What these traditions allow her to do, then, is to take off from their effects and create a radical, modern figure.

When Zilia begins learning how to write French, she is writing to Aza. She justifies learning the language of her captors both by her need to obtain information about her beloved Aza's whereabouts and by her need to place their story within the European landscape. But as Zilia progresses in her mastery of that foreign language, she also sketches out the lines of another story, the story twentieth-century feminist critics like Hélène Cixous have called a coming to writing. "I owe a part of this knowledge," she writes to Aza, "to a kind of writing called *books*" (letter 20). Zilia's fascination here for the wonderful men who have actually written these books helps us understand the ending of the novel. She wonders about the respect writers earn for their contribution to the social good and what rank they occupy in society (letter 22). In the chateau of her own that (magically) becomes her French home, Zilia is especially thrilled by her personal library: "countless books of all colors, shapes, and sizes which were in admirable condition" (letter 35). Zilia can hardly tear herself away to visit the rest of her domain before having read all of them. Though her collection is not likely to rival Montesquieu's real one (nor does she enjoy his seventeen secretaries), it perhaps is competitive with Montaigne's book-lined tower: a privileged place for writing and meditation.

Before Zilia runs out of quipus, she explains to Aza that she was hoping to continue writing to him, even though she doesn't know where he is, in order not only to keep a record of her feelings for him but also to "preserve the memory of this singular nation's principal customs" (letter 16). The first project owes everything to the logic of the sentimental; the second to something less predictable: the performance of cultural criticism. Put another way, these two desires are functions of the two genres intertwined in Graffigny's novel: the love-letter novel and the philosophical tale. Although in conventional literary histories *Letters from a Peruvian Woman* tends to be ranked among "women's novels"—that is, the novels for "sensitive hearts," as if the love story were its only reason for existence—Graffigny's novel should also be understood as part of the philosophical tradition of social analysis through fiction. Or we could say that it offers a critique of both modes.

In one of Zilia's earliest experiences as an observer of this strange nation's customs, she encounters "that ingenious device that duplicates objects" (letter 12). What's interesting about this characteristic use of periphrasis—describing the function of an object in the absence of its proper name—is that it does not lead to a discussion of feminine vanity. When Zilia looks in the mirror, she likes her new French style, but she does not remain fascinated by her image. Although she is surprised to see herself "as if I were standing opposite myself," the discovery becomes the first occasion in which Zilia tries on her new persona as cultural critic: "These marvels disturb the mind and offend reason. What is one to think of this country's inhabitants? Must one fear them? Must one love them? I shall be careful to reserve judgment in this matter" (letter 10). In this mirror stage of self-identification, Zilia learns the power of doubleness. To be double is to understand that identity is always intersubjective.

Like the *précieuses* before her, who were also known for their gift for periphrasis, Zilia's true love turns out to be a passion for the power of language; and there is nothing ridiculous about her desire to learn how to make language empowering for her designs of autonomy. Zilia struggles through her writing lessons—"the method used here to give a kind of existence to thoughts" (letter 16)—in order, she says, to discover the whereabouts of her fiancé and to proclaim her love for him, writing his name, like graffiti, on the walls (letter 18). Although, as it turns out, Zilia's dearest Aza turns out to be unworthy of such devotion and Déterville, the French suitor, arrives too late for a replay of the marriage plot, the writing lessons have not been in vain. By giving a kind of existence to thoughts, writing has given Zilia the possibility of producing novel ideas for her existence.

Graffigny's fiction creates a subversive heroine, who resists in writing the authority of her masters, old and new. But can the "master's tools dismantle the master's house?" Audre Lorde's question is one we should keep in our minds as we reread this eighteenth-century feminist fable. It's a question not unfamiliar to the philosophes themselves.

Nancy K. Miller

Notes

[1]For biographical information on the years 1695–1739 of Graffigny's life, see volume 1 of her *Correspondance*, ed. J. A. Dainard, English Showalter, et al. (Oxford: Voltaire Foundation, 1985) xxv–xxxvii. For later years, the letters themselves must be consulted. Volume 3 of her *Correspondance*, which goes through 1742, appeared in 1992. In the eighteenth century, her name was written both "Grafigny" and

"Graffigny." We follow the decision of the editors of her correspondence: Graffigny.

[2]See David Smith, "The Popularity of Mme de Graffigny's *Lettres d'une Péruvienne*: The Bibliographical Evidence," *Eighteenth-Century Fiction* 3 (1990): 1–20.

[3]See in particular letters 33 and 34. Letters 29 and 34 contain the novel's most unflinching social protest.

[4]The introduction may have been written by Antoine Bret or in collaboration with him.

SELECTED BIBLIOGRAPHY

Altman, Janet Gurkin. "Graffigny's Epistemology and the Emergence of Third-World Ideology." *Writing the Female Voice: Essays on Epistolary Literature*. Ed. Elizabeth C. Goldsmith. Boston: Northeastern UP, 1989.

———. "A Woman's Place in the Enlightenment Sun: The Case of F. de Graffigny." *Romance Quarterly* 38 (1991): 261–71.

DeJean, Joan. *Tender Geographies: Women and the Origins of the Novel in France*. New York: Columbia UP, 1991.

Douthwaite, Julia V. *Exotic Women: Literary Heroines and Cultural Strategies in Ancien Régime France*. Philadelphia: U of Pennsylvania P, 1992.

Jensen, Katharine A. *Writing Love: Letters, Women, and the Novel (1605–1776)*. Carbondale: Southern Illinois UP, 1994.

Landy-Houillon, Isabelle. Introduction. Lettres portugaises, Lettres d'une Péruvienne *et autres romans d'amour par lettres*. Paris: Garnier, 1983.

MacArthur, Elizabeth J. "Devious Narratives: Refusal of Closure in Two Eighteenth-Century Novels." *Eighteenth-Century Studies* 21.1 (1987): 1–20.

Miller, Nancy K. *Subject to Change: Reading Feminist Writing*. New York: Columbia UP, 1988.

Showalter, English, Jr. "Les Lettres d'une Péruvienne: Composition, Publication, Suites." *Archives et Bibliothèques de Belgique* 54.1–4 (1983): 14–28.

Undank, Jack. "Grafigny's Room of Her Own." *French Forum* 13.3 (1988): 297–318.

TRANSLATOR'S NOTE

Where possible, I have preserved the spelling (including discrepancies), capitalization, and italicization of proper nouns used in the French text. The one notable exception is the term for the Peruvian record-keeping device consisting of knotted cords, referred to as "quipos" in the original but given as "quipus" in modern English usage (*Merriam-Webster's Collegiate Dictionary*, 10th ed.).

I have also preserved the paragraphing of the original text except when punctuating dialogue, which I have done in accordance with standard English practice. While doing my best to preserve the original flow and cadence of the original, I have frequently modified punctuation and sentence breaks within paragraphs.

Certain key French words have been translated by the same English word throughout even though the English word has somewhat different connotations. These key words include "tendre" (tender), "tendresse" (tenderness), and "retraite" (retreat).

Unless otherwise indicated, the footnotes are those of the original text. Footnotes I have added are marked with an asterisk. Square brackets enclose translations of the

titles of works cited and any explanatory material I have
added to the original footnotes.

I would like to thank Joseph Gibaldi and Phyllis Franklin for making the MLA Texts and Translations series possible; Nancy K. Miller and Joan DeJean, the editors of the
Graffigny title, for their close reading and constructive
criticism of my translation; English Showalter for sharing
with me his profound knowledge of Françoise de Graffigny's work; Anne-Solange Noble and Renata Morteo for
their help in obtaining permission to use the Flammarion
edition of the French text; Olivier Nora and Nathalie
Duval, my colleagues at the French Publishers' Agency,
for being patient with my absences to work on this translation and for providing a native French speaker's perspective on the most difficult passages in the text; and, most
of all, M. Janet Harris for her invaluable intellectual and
moral support.

David Kornacker

FRANÇOISE DE GRAFFIGNY

Letters from a
Peruvian Woman

Foreword

While truth that diverges from the plausible generally loses its credibility in the eyes of reason, this loss is not irrevocable; but should truth run even slightly counter to prejudice, it will rarely find favor before that tribunal. What is there, then, that the publisher of this work should not fear in presenting to the public the letters of a young woman of Peru whose manner of writing and thinking has so little relation to the rather unfavorable opinion of her nation that an unjust prejudice has caused us to form?

Enriched by the valuable spoils of Peru, we should at the very least view the inhabitants of that part of the world as a magnificent people, and the feeling of respect is hardly far removed from the notion of magnificence.

But ever predisposed in our own favor, we acknowledge merit in other nations only to the extent that their customs imitate our own, that their tongue resembles our language. How can one be Persian?[1]

We look down on Indians, barely acknowledging that these unfortunate peoples possess a thinking soul, yet their history is readily accessible to everyone, and throughout that history we find monuments to the wisdom of their spirit and soundness of their philosophy.

---

[1] *Lettres persanes* [Montesquieu, *Persian Letters*, trans. C. J. Betts (London: Penguin, 1973) 83].

3

One of our greatest poets sketched Indian customs in a dramatic poem that has surely helped make them better known.[2]

Because the light of so much learning has already been shed on these peoples' character, it would seem that one should not fear seeing original letters treated as fiction when they serve only to develop further what we already know of the Indians' lively and natural spirit. But does prejudice have eyes? Nothing ensures against its judgment, and we would certainly not have submitted this work to it were its dominion without bounds.

It would seem unnecessary to indicate that the first letters have been translated by Zilia herself: since they were composed in a language and recorded in a manner that are both equally unknown to us, the reader will readily surmise that the letters making up this collection would not have reached us had not the same hand written them in our language.

We owe this translation to Zilia's leisure in her retreat. Because she was obliging enough to give these letters to the Chevalier Déterville and he obtained her permission to keep them, they have come down to us.

The grammatical errors and lapses in style of these letters will allow one easily to recognize how scrupulous we have been about preserving the ingenuousness of

---

[2]*Alzire* [a tragedy by Voltaire, first performed in 1736].

spirit that predominates in this work. We have limited ourselves to taking out many figures of speech not in use in our style, leaving in only the number necessary to let it be felt how many had to be removed.

We also believed ourselves able, without changing any of the content of the thought, to give a more intelligible cast to certain metaphysical utterances which might otherwise have seemed obscure. That is the only part we have in this singular work.

Historical Introduction
to *Letters from a Peruvian Woman*

There is no other people whose knowledge of their origins and antiquity is as limited as that of the Peruvians. Their annals barely contain the history of four centuries.

Mancocapac, according to these people's traditions, was their law giver and first Inca. He said that the Sun (which they called their father and viewed as their God), moved by the barbarism in which they had long been living, sent them from Heaven two of his children, a son and a daughter, to give them laws and to urge them, by establishing cities and tending the earth, to become rational men.

Thus, it is to *Mancocapac* and his wife *Coya-Mama-Oello-Huaco* that the Peruvians owe the principles, customs, and arts that had made of them a happy people when avarice, coming from the heart of a world whose very existence they never suspected, cast upon their lands tyrants whose barbarity became the shame of humanity and the crime of their century.

The circumstances in which the Peruvians found themselves at the time the Spaniards landed could not have been more favorable to the Iberians. For some time there had been talk of an ancient oracle proclaiming that *after a certain number of kings, to their land would come extraordinary men such as had never been seen, who would invade their realm and destroy their religion.*

Although astronomy was one of the Peruvians' principal areas of knowledge, they, like so many other peoples, took fright at natural wonders. Three circles that had been observed around the moon, and especially a few comets, had spread terror among them. Everything—an eagle pursued by other birds, the sea overflowing its banks—everything made the oracle as infallible as it was deadly.

The oldest son of the seventh of the Incas, whose name in the Peruvian language foretold the fatality of his era,[3] had once seen a man of a figure quite different from that of a Peruvian. This specter had a long beard, a robe that covered its legs down to the feet, and led an unknown animal by a tether, all of which had frightened the young prince, to whom this phantom had said that he was son of the Sun, brother of *Mancocapac*, and that his name was Viracocha. Unfortunately, this ridiculous fable had been preserved among the Peruvians, so the moment they saw the Spaniards with their long beards and covered legs mounted on animals the likes of which they had never known, they believed themselves to be seeing in them the sons of this Viracocha who had proclaimed himself son of the Sun. It was for this reason that the usurper had himself given by the ambassadors he sent them the title descendant of the God they worshipped. All bowed down before them, for people are the same everywhere. The

---

[3]He was named *Yahuarhuocac*, which literally means *Weep-blood*.

Spaniards were acclaimed all but unanimously as Gods whose rage even the most lavish offerings and humiliating homages could not assuage.

Having noticed that the Spaniards' horses chomped their bits, the Peruvians believed that these tamed monsters, who shared in their respect and perhaps their worship as well, fed on metal. Accordingly, they went and fetched all the gold and silver they possessed for the horses, surrounding them each day with these offerings. We limit ourselves to this detail to paint a picture of the natives' credulity and of how easy the Spaniards found it to seduce them.

Whatever homage the Peruvians might have paid their tyrants, they had allowed their great riches to show too much to obtain any leniency from them.

An entire people, subjugated and begging for mercy, was put to the sword. Violation of all human rights left the Spaniards absolute masters of the treasures of one of the most beautiful parts of the world. "Base and mechanical victories!" cried Montaigne,[4] recalling the vile purpose of those conquests, then added, "Never did ambition, never did public enmities, drive men against one another to such horrible hostilities and such miserable calamaties."

---

[4]Tome V, chap. vi, des Coches ["Of Coaches," *The Complete Essays of Montaigne*, trans. Donald M. Frame (Stanford: Stanford UP, 1957) 695; bk. 3, essay 6].

Thus were the Peruvians made the sad victims of a greedy people who at first showed them only good faith and even friendship. Ignorance of our vices and the naive nature of their customs flung them into the arms of their venal enemies. For naught had vast spaces separated the cities of the Sun from our world: they became its prey and most precious dominion.

What a spectacle for the Spaniards must the gardens of the temple of the Sun have been, where the trees, fruits, and flowers were of gold worked with a skill unknown in Europe! The gold-plated walls of the temple, countless statues covered with precious stones, and many other riches previously unknown dazzled the conquerors of that unfortunate people. While giving free reign to their cruelty, they forgot that the Peruvians were men.

An exposition of the mores of those unfortunate peoples as brief as the one just given of their misfortunes will conclude the introduction it was thought necessary to add to the Letters that follow.

In general those peoples were open and humane; their attachment to their religion made them strict observers of laws they viewed as the work of *Mancocapac*, son of the Sun they worshipped.

Although that star was the lone God to whom they had built temples, they recognized a God of creation above him whom they called *Pachacamac*. For them, this was the *great name*. The word Pachacamac was uttered but rarely, and with signs of the utmost admiration. They also had a great deal of reverence for the Moon, which they treated as the Sun's wife and sister. They regarded the Moon as the mother of all things, but like all Indians, they believed that she would bring about the destruction of the world by allowing herself to drop onto the earth, which she would annihilate by her fall. Thunder, which they called *Yalpor*, and lightning passed among them for ministers of the Sun's justice, and this notion contributed more than a little to the sacred respect inspired in them by the first Spaniards, whose firearms they took for instruments of thunder.

A belief in the immortality of the soul was well established among the Peruvians. They believed, as do the majority of Indians, that the soul journeys to places unknown where it is rewarded or punished as it deserves.

Their offerings to the Sun were composed of gold and all their most precious possessions. *Raymi* was this God's principal feast at which offerings of *maïs* were made in a goblet. This *maïs* was a kind of strong liquor the Peruvians knew how to extract from one of their plants, which they drank to the point of inebriation after making their sacrifices.

There were one hundred doors in the superb temple of the Sun. Only the ruling Inca, called the Capa-Inca, possessed the right to have them opened. It was also his right alone to penetrate the temple's inner sanctum.

The Virgins consecrated to the Sun were raised there practically from birth and maintained a perpetual virginity under the supervision of their *Mamas*, or governesses, unless the laws should destine them to marry Incas, who were obliged always to wed their sisters or, lacking sisters, the first princess of the blood who was a Virgin of the Sun. One of the principal occupations of these Virgins was fashioning the Incas' diadems, whose entire richness derived from a kind of fringe.

The temple was decorated with the various idols of the peoples subjugated by the Incas after having first been made to accept the worship of the Sun. The sumptuousness of the metals and precious stones embellishing it endowed it with a magnificence and splendor worthy of the God served there.

The obedience and respect of the Peruvians for their kings was based on their belief that the Sun was the father of those kings. But the fondness and love they felt for them was the fruit of their own virtues, and of the Incas' fairness.

Young people were brought up with all the care required by the happy simplicity of their moral beliefs. Subordination in no way frightened their minds because its necessity was demonstrated to them early on and because neither tyranny nor vainglory had any part in it. Modesty and mutual consideration were the cornerstones of their child rearing. Those who were assigned this task were careful to correct their charges' first failings and to halt the progress of any budding passions,[5] or to divert them to the benefit of society. There are certain virtues that imply many others. To give some idea of the Peruvians', suffice it to say that before the landing of the Spaniards, it was taken for granted that no Peruvian had ever lied.

The *Amautas*, that nation's version of our philosophes, taught the young of the discoveries made in the sciences. Their nation was still in its infancy in that respect but in the prime of its happiness.

The Peruvians were less enlightened than we are, possessing less knowledge and fewer skills than we do, and yet they had enough of these not to want for any of the essentials. Their *quapas*, or *quipus*,[6] replaced for them our art of writing. Cords of cotton or gut to which other cords of different colors were attached reminded them by means of knots placed at different distances of those things they wished to remember. These *quipus* served them as annals and codes, were used at their rituals and

---

[5]See the descriptions of religious ceremonies and customs in *Dissertations sur les peuples de l'Amérique* ["Essays on the Peoples of the Americas"], chap. 13. [If any work with the title given here ever existed, it was extremely obscure. English Showalter suggests that the information may in fact have been drawn from J.-F. Bernard, Antoine-Augustin Bruzen de La Martinière, et al., *Cérémonies et coutumes religieuses de tous les peuples du monde* 'Religious Ceremonies and Customs of All the Peoples of the World' (Amsterdam, 1723 43), 8 vols.]

[6]The quipus of Peru were also in use among several other peoples of the southern Americas.

ceremonies, and so on. They had public officials called *Quipucamaios*, to whose care the *quipus* were entrusted. The state treasury, financial records, tribute payments—indeed, all business dealings and all reckoning—were handled as easily with *quipus* as they could have been using writing.

The wise lawgiver of Peru, Mancocapac, had made sacred the tending of the land. It was conducted communally, and the days devoted to this work were days of celebration. Canals of prodigious expanse distributed freshness and fertility to all parts of their lands. But what is scarcely conceivable is that without any tools of iron or steel, hence by brute strength alone, the Peruvians were able to overturn boulders and cross the highest mountains so as to put in their superb aquaducts, as well as the roads they built throughout the country.

In Peru they knew as much geometry as was needed to measure and divide land. Medicine was a science unknown to them, though they did make use of certain secrets for a few special kinds of accidents. *Garcilasso** said that they had a sort of music and even some manner of poetry. Their poets, whom they called *Hasavec*, wrote works not unlike tragedies and comedies that the sons of

---

*TRANSLATOR'S NOTE: The reference is to Garcilaso de la Vega, El Inca (c. 1539–1616), the son of Pizarro's lieutenant Sebastián Garcilaso de la Vega y Vargas and an Inca princess. His works on Inca customs and history were widely available in eighteenth-century France.

14

the *Caciques*[7] and the *Curacas*[8] staged before the Incas and the rest of the court on feast days.

Thus, morals and the knowledge of those laws favoring the good of society were the only things that the Peruvians had learned with any degree of success. According to one historian,[9] it must be acknowledged that "[t]heir deeds were so great, and their rule so good that few in the world have bettered them."

---

[7]Caciques, a kind of provincial magistrate.

[8]Rulers of a small district; they never appeared before the Incas and their queens without offering them as tribute a sampling of the curiosities produced by the province under their command.

[9]Puffendorf, *Introd. à l'Histoire* ["Introduction to History"]. [The author's full name is most commonly given as Samuel, Freiherr von Pufendorf (1632–94). Pufendorf's work covers only Europe. For the seven-volume 1738 edition of the work that Graffigny has in mind (Amsterdam: Zacharie Chatelain), Antoine-Augustin Bruzen de La Martinière wrote a two-volume continuation entitled *Introduction à l'histoire de l'Asie, de l'Afrique, et de l'Amérique. Pour servir de suite à l'Introduction à l'histoire du Baron de Pufendorff* 'Introduction to the History of Asia, Africa, and America. To Serve as a Continuation to Baron de Pufendorff's *Introduction to History*.' La Martinière summarizes Garcilaso de la Vega in volume 2, chapter 7, but does not include the quotation for which the work is cited. The quotation is in fact taken verbatim from Garcilaso's *Histoire des Yncas* (Paris: Prault, 1744) 2: 59, where it is part of a long passage attributed to Piedro Cieça de Leon. The English translation quoted here is from Garcilaso de la Vega, El Inca, *Royal Commentaries of the Incas and General History of Peru*, trans. and introd. Harold V. Livermore, foreword by Arnold J. Toynbee (Austin: U of Texas P, 1966) 91, where the attribution is to Piedro Cieza de Léon.]

15

I

Aza, my dear Aza! Like a morning mist the cries of your[*]
tender Zilia rise up and have dissipated before reaching
you. In vain do I call to you for help, in vain do I wait for
you to come and break the bonds of my enslavement.
But alas, perhaps those misfortunes of which I remain
unaware are the most dreadful! Perhaps your woes surpass mine!

The city of the Sun, offered up to the fury of a barbarous nation, should make my tears flow, yet my
sorrow, my fears, and my despair are only for you.

What did you do amid that dreadful tumult, dear soul
of my life? Was your courage harmful or useless to you?
Cruel alternatives! Mortal worry! Oh dearest Aza, may
your days be saved and may I succumb, if need be, to the
weight of my afflictions!

From that terrible moment (which should have been
torn from the chain of time and resubmerged in the eternal store of ideas), that moment of horror when those
term impious savages stole me away from the worship of the
would Sun, from myself, and from your love, I have experienced
beg nothing save the effects of unhappiness without being
used able to discover their cause, held as I am in strict captivity,
by
Euro. denied all communication with our citizens, and not
about
her.

---

[*]TRANSLATOR'S NOTE: Aza is the only character in the novel with
whom Zilia uses the informal second-person "tu" and its correspond-
ing forms.

17

knowing the language of these ferocious men whose bonds I bear. I am submerged in an abyss of darkness, and my days resemble the most frightening of nights.

Far from being moved by my entreaties, my abductors are not even touched by my tears; deaf to my language, they understand no better the cries of my despair.

What people is so ferocious as to be unmoved by signs of pain? What arid desert witnessed the birth of humans insensitive to the voice of nature groaning? These barbarous masters of *Yalpor*,[10] proud of their power to exterminate, are guided in their actions by cruelty alone! Oh Aza, how will you escape their fury? Where are you? What are you doing? If my life is dear to you, advise me of your fate.

Alas, how mine has changed! How can it be that days so similar one to another should be so woefully different in relation to us? Time passes, shadows succeed the light, no disturbance is to be perceived in nature, yet I have fallen from the heights of happiness into the depths of horror and despair without any mediating interval to prepare me for this ghastly passage.

You well know, oh delight of my heart, that this horrible day, forever frightful, was to have shone upon the triumph of our union! Hardly had it commenced to dawn when, impatient to carry out a project that my tender-

---

[10]The name for thunder.

ness had inspired in me during the night, I ran to my *quipus*[11] and, taking advantage of the silence that still prevailed in the temple, hastened to knot them in the hope that with their help I might immortalize the story of our love and happiness.

As I worked, the undertaking seemed less difficult to me; moment by moment that countless heap of cords turned beneath my fingers into a faithful depiction of our actions and feelings, as in other times it had been the interpreter of our thoughts during the long intervals we went without seeing each other.

Entirely absorbed in my endeavor, I lost all track of time, when suddenly sounds of commotion brought me back to my senses and made my heart quiver.

I thought that the happy moment had arrived and that the one hundred doors[12] were being opened to give free passage to the Sun of my days. I hastily hid my *quipus* under a fold of my dress and raced toward the sound of your steps.

But what a horrible sight met my eye! The dreadful memory of it will never be erased from my mind.

---

[11]A great number of short cords of different colors that the Indians used for lack of writing to pay soldiers and count population. Some authors claim that they also used them to pass on to posterity the memorable actions of their Incas.

[12]There were one hundred doors to the temple of the Sun; only the *Inca* possessed the right to have them opened.

The bloodied paving stones of the temple, the trampled image of the Sun, raging soldiers chasing down our distraught Virgins and massacring all that stood in their way, our *Mamas*[13] dying beneath their blows in clothes still burning from the fire of their thunder, and the groans of terror and cries of fury from every direction spreading horror and fear combined to take my very senses from me.

When I came to, I found that by a natural and all but involuntary movement I had placed myself behind the altar, which I held in a tight embrace. Paralyzed with fear, indeed not even breathing lest I be noticed, I saw those barbarians pass by.

While so doing, I noticed that they were slowing the manifestations of their cruelty at the sight of the precious ornaments spread throughout the temple, that they seized those whose glitter most struck them, and that they were tearing the very gold plate from the walls. I judged that thievery was the motive for their barbarity and that by not opposing their actions I might escape their blows. I planned to leave the temple, have myself conducted to your palace, and request of the *Capa Inca*[14] aid and refuge for me and my companions. But as soon as I made the first move to slip away, I felt myself being detained. Oh dearest Aza, I still shudder at the thought:

---

[13]A kind of governess for the Virgins of the Sun.
[14]Generic term for reigning Incas.

those impious men dared to lay their sacrilegious hands on the daughter of the Sun!

Torn from the sacred dwelling, ignominiously dragged outside the temple, I saw for the first time the threshold of the celestial door that I was only supposed to cross bearing the adornments of royalty.[15] Instead of the flowers that would have been strewn at my feet, I saw the streets covered with blood and dying people; instead of enjoying the honors of the throne I was to share with you, I find myself enslaved to tyranny, held captive in a dark prison, the space I occupy in the universe limited to the confines of my being. A mat bathed in my tears receives my body, wearied by the torments of my soul. But how light so many woes will be to me, dear pillar of my life, if I learn that you still breathe!

Amid all this dreadful upheaval, I have, by some happy chance, managed to preserve my *quipus*. I have them, dearest Aza! Today they are my heart's sole treasure, for they shall serve as interpreter for your love as for mine. The same knots that will inform you of my existence shall, by changing form in your hands, tell me of your fate. But alas, by what means will I be able to convey them to you? By what deft artifice might they be returned to me? I still know not, but the same spirit that caused us to invent their use will suggest to us the means

---

[15] Virgins consecrated to the Sun entered the temple practically at birth and only left it on the day of their marriage.

21

of fooling our tyrants. I will not stop envying the good fortune of whatever faithful *Chaqui*[16] is entrusted with conveying this precious package to you. He will see you, dearest Aza, and I would give all the days the Sun has allotted me to enjoy one single moment of your presence. He will see you, dearest Aza! The sound of your voice will strike respect and fear in his soul. It would bring joy and happiness to mine. He will see you and, certain that you are alive, he will bless your life in your presence, while I, abandoned to uncertainty, will feel my impatience for his return dry up the blood in my veins. Dearest Aza, all the torments of tender souls are assembled in my heart! Seeing you for a moment would dispel them: I would give my life to enjoy that delight.

II

Dearest Aza, may the tree of virtue forever shade the family of the pious citizen who received beneath my window the mysterious weaving recording my thoughts and placed it in your hands! May *Pachammac*[17] extend the number of his years as a reward for his deftness in having passed to me the divine pleasures accompanying your reply!

The treasures of Love are open to me; I draw from them an exquisite pleasure that intoxicates my soul. As I unravel the secrets of your heart, mine bathes in a per-

---

[16]Messenger.
[17]The God of creation, more powerful than the Sun.

fumed sea. You live, and the chains that were to unite us have not been broken! Such great happiness was the object of my desires, not my hopes.

In surrendering my person, I feared only for your life; now that I know it to be safe, I no longer see the misfortune. You love me, and shattered joy is reborn in my heart. I thrill to taste the delicious confidence of pleasing that which I love; but this confidence in no way causes me to forget that it is to you I owe all that you deign to find appealing in me. Just as the rose draws its brilliant color from the rays of the Sun, so the charms you find in my heart and mind are only the beneficial effects of your luminous genius; nothing is mine save my tenderness.

If you were an ordinary man, I would have remained in the ignorance to which my sex is condemned; but your soul was above those customs and regarded them as nothing other than abuse. You broke down their barriers to raise me up to you. You could not tolerate that a being similar to your own should be limited to the humiliating advantage of giving life to your posterity. You wanted our divine *Amautas*[18] to embellish my understanding with their sublime knowledge. But without the desire to please you, oh light of my life, would I have been capable of resolving to give up my blissful ignorance for the painful occupation of study? Without the desire to merit

---

[18]Indian philosophes.

your esteem, your confidence, and your respect by means of virtues that fortify love and that love then transforms into pleasure, I would only be the object of your eyes, and absence would already have erased me from your memory.

Alas, if you still love me, why am I enslaved? As I cast my gaze against the walls of my prison, my joy disappears, horror grips me, and my fears are renewed. Your liberty has not been taken from you, yet you do not come to my rescue; you know of my fate, yet it remains unchanged. No, dearest Aza, these ferocious peoples whom you call Spaniards have not left you as free as you think you are. I see as many signs of enslavement in the honors they heap upon you as in the captivity in which they keep me.

Your goodness leads you astray; you believe the promises these barbarians have their interpreter make to you to be sincere because your own word is inviolable. But I who do not understand their language, I whom they do not think worth deceiving, I see their actions.

Your subjects take them for gods and go over to their side. Oh my dear Aza, woe unto the people ruled by fear! Save yourself from that error, beware the false kindness of strangers. Give up your empire, for *Viracocha* has foretold its destruction. Buy back your life and your freedom at the price of your power, your grandeur, your riches.

Your natural gifts will be all that remains to you, and our days will be safe.

Rich in the possession of our hearts, great through our virtues, powerful in our moderation, we shall go live in a hut and draw our pleasure from the sky, the earth, and our tenderness. You will be more of a king ruling over my soul than you are doubting the affection of a countless people. My submission to your wishes will allow you to enjoy without tyranny the noble right to command. As I obey you, I shall make your empire echo with the sound of my songs of joy; your diadem[19] will always be the work of my hands; of your royalty you will lose only the cares and sorrows.

How many times, dear soul of my life, have you complained of the responsibilities of your rank! How greatly did the ceremonies accompanying your visits make you envy the lot of your subjects! You would have wished to live only for me, yet you would now fear to shed so many constraints? Am I no longer that Zilia whom you would have preferred to your empire? No, I cannot believe it; my heart is utterly unchanged, so why should yours be?

I still see and love the same Aza who has ruled my soul from the first moment I saw him. I remember that fortunate day when your father, my sovereign lord, brought

---

[19]The diadem of the Incas was a kind of fringed braid woven by the Virgins of the Sun.

you to share for the first time in the power, reserved to him alone, of entering the temple's inner sanctum.[20] I picture the pleasant spectacle of our Virgins assembled, their beauty all the more lustrous for the charming order in which they were arranged, just as the most brilliant flowers in a garden are even more spectacular for the symmetry of their beds.

You appeared in our midst like the rising Sun, whose tender light prepares the way for the serenity of a beautiful day. The fire of your eyes colored our cheeks with the hue of modesty, and an ingenuous confusion held our gazes captive. Yours was bright with joy: you had never encountered so many beauties assembled. We had seen no man save the *Capa-Inca*. An astonished silence prevailed. I do not know what thoughts went through the minds of my fellow Virgins, but by what feelings was my heart not assailed! For the first time I felt distress, agitation, and yet pleasure. Confounded by the upheaval in my soul, I was about to flee from your sight, but you walked toward me and respect held me back.

Oh my dear Aza, the memory of that first moment of my happiness will always be dear to me! The sound of your voice along with the melodious singing of our hymns sent coursing through my veins the sweet shud-

---

[20]The reigning Inca alone had the right to enter the temple of the Sun.

der and sacred respect that the presence of the Divinity inspires in us.

Shaking and awestruck, I found that timidity had left me unable even to speak. Emboldened at last by the gentleness of your words, I dared raise my eyes to look upon you, and our gazes met. No, not even death itself will ever erase from my memory the tender movement of our souls as they met and became as one in the space of an instant.

If we could have had any doubts as to our origins, dearest Aza, that ray of light would have confounded our uncertainty, for what other than the principle of fire could have placed in us that keen understanding of each other's hearts, an understanding that was communicated, absorbed, and felt with inexplicable rapidity?

I was too ignorant of the effects of love not to be fooled. Because my imagination was filled with the sublime theology of our *Cucipatas*,[21] I took the flame that consumed me for a divine visitation; I thought that the Sun was showing me his will through you and that he was choosing me to be his elite spouse.[22] I yearned to be so chosen, but after you departed, I examined my heart and found only your image in it.

Dearest Aza, what a change your presence had brought over me! All objects looked new to me; I felt I was seeing

---

[21]Sun priests.
[22]One Virgin, chosen by the Sun, was never to be married.

27

my fellow Virgins for the first time. How beautiful they looked to me! I could not bear their presence. Standing off to one side, I was abandoning myself to the contemplation of my troubled soul when one of them came to draw me from my reverie only to give me new reason to return to it, for she informed me that, as your closest female relative, I was to be your wife as soon as my age would permit our union.

I did not know the laws of your empire,[23] but from the moment I had seen you, my heart was too enlightened not to comprehend the idea of the happiness of belonging to you. And yet, far from grasping the true breadth of that happiness and still accustomed to the sacred name of wife of the Sun, I limited my hopes to seeing you every day, adoring you, and offering you vows as I offered them to the Sun.

It was you, dearest Aza, you who then filled my soul with delight by informing me that the august rank of your wife would link me to your heart, your throne, your glory, your virtues; that I would enjoy without cease those moments together, so rare and so brief, as often as we should desire, moments that adorned my mind with the perfections of your soul and added to my happiness the delicious hope of one day being the cause of yours.

---

[23]Indian law required Incas to marry their sisters or, if they had no sister, to take as their wife the first princess of Inca blood who was a Sun Virgin.

Oh dearest Aza, how flattering to my heart was your impatience at my extreme youth, which delayed our union. How long those two intervening years have seemed to you, yet how short they were! Alas, the long awaited moment had arrived. What ill-fortune rendered it so fateful? What God hounds innocence and virtue in such a way? Or what infernal power has separated us from ourselves? Horror grips me, my heart is torn asunder, tears soak my handiwork. Aza! My dear Aza! . . .

III

It is you, dear light of my days, you who call me back to life. Would I wish to preserve my own were I not certain that death would have reaped at one stroke your days and mine! I was reaching the point where the spark of the divine fire by which the Sun animates our being was going to be extinguished. Ever toiling nature was already preparing to give another form to that share of matter in me that belongs to it: I was dying, and you were losing forever half of your very self, when my love gave me back my life, and I make of it an offering to you. But how could I possibly explain to you the surprising things that have happened to me? How can I organize thoughts that were already confused at the moment I was having them and have been rendered even less intelligible by the time that has since passed?

29

Oh dearest Aza, scarcely had I entrusted the last strand of my thoughts to our faithful *Chaqui* when I heard a great commotion in our dwelling. In the middle of the night, two of my abductors came and removed me from my dark retreat, using as much violence as they had to tear me from the temple of the Sun.

I know not down what path they led me. We traveled only by night, and during the day we stopped in arid deserts without seeking any retreat. Soon succumbing to fatigue, I was then carried in some manner of *Hamas*, whose movements tired me almost as much as walking would have. At last we apparently reached our intended destination, for one night those barbarians picked me up and carried me into a house that, despite the darkness, I sensed to be extremely difficult to approach. I was put in an even more cramped and uncomfortable place than my first cell had ever been. But, dearest Aza, could I convince you of what I fail to understand myself, were you not certain that a lie has never sullied the lips of a child of the Sun![24] That house, which I had judged to be quite large by virtue of the number of people it held, was as if suspended, for, having no contact with the earth, it was in a perpetual rocking motion.

Understanding this wonder, oh light of my mind, would have required that *Ticaiviracocha* have filled my

---

[24]It was taken for granted that no Peruvian had ever lied.

soul as he did yours with his divine wisdom. All I know of it is that this dwelling was not built by a being friendly to men, for a few moments after I entered it, its continual motion combined with a noxious odor caused me to feel so ill that I am amazed not to have succumbed to my malady. This was but the beginning of my troubles.

A rather long period of time had passed, and I hardly suffered anymore, when one morning I was torn from my sleep by a sound more frightful than that of *Yalpa*. Our dwelling was being shaken by tremors such as the earth will experience when the moon, by falling, reduces the universe to dust.[25] Shouts, which were added to this din, made it even more frightful; my senses, paralyzed by a secret horror, conveyed to my soul only the idea of nature's utter destruction. I thought the peril to be universal and feared for your life. My terror finally reached its very highest point at the sight of a troop of raging men, their faces and clothes covered with blood, who came crashing into my room. Unable to bear that horrible spectacle, I lost all strength of body and consciousness of mind. I am still ignorant of what followed that terrible event. When I came to, I found myself in a reasonably clean bed surrounded by several savages who were no longer those cruel Spaniards but who were no less unknown to me.

---

[25]The Indians believed that the end of the world would be brought about by the moon's letting itself drop onto the earth.

Can you imagine my surprise at finding myself in a new dwelling, among new men, without being able to understand how this change could have come to pass? I promptly closed my eyes so that, having gathered my wits about me, I might determine if I was alive or if my soul might not have left my body and crossed over to the unknown regions.[26]

I will confess to you, dear idol of my heart, that, tired of a hateful existence, disheartened by having to suffer torments of all kinds, overwhelmed by the weight of my horrible fate, I looked with indifference upon what I sensed to be my life's approaching end and consistently refused whatever aid was offered me. In the course of a few days I reached the fatal limit and came to that point without regret.

Exhausting one's strength obliterates feeling. Already my weakened imagination received images as nothing more than vague sketches drawn by a trembling hand; already objects that had once affected me the most now elicited from me nothing save that vague sensation we feel when allowing our minds to wander in formless reverie. I almost was no more. That state, dearest Aza, is not as unpleasant as one thinks. From a distance it frightens us because we think upon it in possession of all our strength, but when we reach that state, weakened by the

---

[26]Indians believed that after death, the soul journeys to places unknown where it is rewarded or punished as it deserves.

gradations of pain and sorrow that have brought us to it, that decisive moment seems no more than one of rest. And yet I could feel that the natural tendency that prompts us, during our lives, to delve ever deeper into the future, even when that future will no longer be for us, seems to find new strength at the moment of life's being lost. One ceases to live for oneself, instead wanting to know how one will live through what one loves. It was in the course of one of those hallucinations of my soul that I thought myself transported inside your palace. I arrived at the very moment you had just been informed of my death. My imagination painted so vividly for me what surely would happen that the truth itself would not have had more power. Dearest Aza, I saw you pale, disfigured, and lifeless, like a lily withered by the searing heat of the midday Sun. Is love then barbarous at times? I rejoiced at your sorrow, stimulating it further with sad farewells. I found some sweetness and perhaps even pleasure in spreading over your days the poison of regrets, and this same love that was making a beast of me tore open my heart with the horror of your woes. At last, awakened as from a deep sleep, cut to the quick by your own pain, fearing for your life, I asked for help and again saw the light.

Will I ever see you again, dear arbiter of my existence? Alas, who can assure me of that? I no longer know where I am; perhaps it is far from you. But should we be separated by the vast spaces inhabited by the children of the Sun, the light cloud of my thoughts shall ceaselessly fly about you all the same.

IV

However great one's love of life, dearest Aza, suffering diminishes it, and despair extinguishes it. First the scorn that nature seems to manifest for our being in abandoning it to pain outrages us; then the impossibility of delivering ourselves from that pain brings us such acute awareness of our humiliating inadequacy that it brings us to the point of disgust with ourselves.

I no longer live in myself or for myself. Every instant in which I draw breath is a sacrifice I make for love of you, and with each passing day it becomes more arduous. While time eases somewhat the violence of the pain that devours me, it redoubles my mind's suffering. Far from clarifying my fate, it seems to make it even murkier. All that surrounds me is unfamiliar, all is new to me. Everything stirs my curiosity, and nothing can satisfy it. It is in vain that I pay attention and make an effort to understand or be understood, since both are equally impossible for me. Tired of so much wasted effort, I thought I could eliminate its source by concealing from my eyes the impressions they received from objects, and for a time I steadfastly kept them shut. Fruitless struggle! The willed shadows to which I had condemned myself soothed only my modesty, ever wounded by the sight of those men whose aid and comfort are so much torture to me; but my soul remained no less restless. Being shut up inside myself only made my anxieties keener and the desire to express them more urgent. The impossibility of making myself understood spreads to my very organs an agony no less intolerable than pains having more evident reality. How cruel is this predicament!

Alas, I thought myself already to be understanding a few of the words of those savage Spaniards. I had found some similarities with our own august language and flattered myself to think that in a short while I would be able to explain myself to them. I am far from enjoying the same advantages in regard to my new tyrants, for they express themselves so rapidly that I cannot even distinguish the inflections of their voices. Everything leads me to believe that they are not from the same nation, and judging by the differences in their manners and their seeming characters, one soon realizes that *Pachacamac* allotted them very different portions of those elements from which he formed human beings. The dark, wild look of my first abductors indicates that they are composed of the stuff of the hardest metals, whereas my current captors seem to have slipped from the hands of the Creator at a time when he had gathered for their composition only air and fire. The proud eyes and dark and tranquil visages of the Spaniards indicated clearly enough that they were cold-blooded in their cruelty, and the inhumanity of their actions bore this out only too well. As for these new ones, their smiling countenances, the kindness of their gaze, and a certain general attentiveness about their actions, seemingly motivated by good will, all argue in their favor, yet I notice contradictions in their behavior that cause me to suspend judgment.

Two of the new savages hardly ever leave my bedside. I believe one, whom I surmise to be the *Cacique*[27] judging by his air of grandeur, to be showing me, after his fashion, a great deal of respect. The other is giving me some portion of the care required by my illness, but his goodness is hard, his aid cruel, and his familiarity imperious.

From that first moment when, having regained some strength, I found myself in their power, that first one, whom I have clearly noticed to be bolder than the others, endeavored to take my hand, which I withdrew from him in a state of unspeakable consternation. He appeared surprised by my resistance and, with no regard for modesty, immediately grasped it again. Weak, faint, and speaking only words that went utterly uncomprehended, could I prevent his doing so? He held my hand, dearest Aza, so long as he wished to, and thenceforth I have had to give it to him myself several times a day if I wish to avoid arguments that always turn to my disadvantage.

---

[27] A *Cacique* is a kind of provincial magistrate.

They conduct a kind of ceremony[28] that seems to me to be a superstition of these peoples: I believe that they find it to have some relation to my ills, but apparently it is necessary to be of their nation to feel the effects, for I have experienced precious few and suffer still from an internal fire that consumes me and leaves me with barely enough strength to knot my *quipus*. I spend as much time on this activity as my weakened state can allow me. These knots strike my senses and seem to lend greater reality to my thoughts. The kind of likeness I imagine they bear to words gives me an illusion that tricks my pain, for I believe myself to be speaking to you, telling you that I love you, reassuring you of my devotion and tenderness. This sweet error is my one possession and my life. If the weight of my burdens forces me to interrupt my work, I groan at your absence; thus, entirely given over to my tenderness, I spend nary a moment that does not belong to you.

Alas, what other use could I put them to? Oh my dearest Aza! Were you not the master of my soul, should the chains of love not bond me inseparably to you, even then, plunged in an abyss of darkness, could I turn my thoughts away from the light of my life? You are the Sun of my days, you brighten and prolong them, they are

---

[28]The Indians had no knowledge of medicine.

yours. You cherish me, I agree to live. What will you do for me? You will love me, and I am repaid.

V

How I have suffered, dearest Aza, since tying the last knots I devoted to you! Being deprived of my *quipus* was still lacking from the sum total of my pains. As soon as my meddlesome persecutors noticed that this work increased my despondency, they denied me its practice.

The treasure of my tenderness was finally restored to me, but it cost me quite a few tears. All that is left me is this manner of expressing my feelings, the sad consolation of painting you a picture of my sorrows. Could I lose that consolation and not despair?

My strange fate has robbed me of everything down to the pleasure that the unfortunate take in recounting their troubles. We believe ourselves to be receiving sympathy when we are heard, a portion of our pain flashes across the faces of those who listen to us, and, for whatever reason, this seems to comfort us. I cannot make myself understood, and good cheer is all about me.

I cannot even enjoy in peace the novel sort of desert to which my inability to communicate my thoughts has consigned me, for I am surrounded by bothersome objects whose attentive gazes disturb my soul's solitude, constrain my body's postures, and inhibit my very thoughts. Indeed, I often find myself forgetting that happy freedom nature granted us by making our feelings impenetrable to others and fear at times that those curious savages might divine the disobliging reflections inspired in me by their strange behavior, to the point that I strain to curb my thoughts as if they could read my mind in spite of me.

One moment destroys the opinion another had given me of their character and their way of thinking in regard to me.

In addition to a countless number of petty refusals, they deny me, dearest Aza, the very nourishments necessary to sustain life, the very freedom to choose the place where I wish to be. By means of a form of violence they hold me in this bed, now grown intolerable to me. Hence, I must believe that they regard me as their slave and that their power is tyrannical.

On the other hand, if I reflect upon the extreme desire they manifest to preserve my life and the respect that accompanies the services they render me, I am tempted to think that they take me for a being of a species superior to humanity.

None of them appears before me without bending more or less deeply at the waist, as we are accustomed to do when praying to the Sun. The *Cacique* seems to want to imitate the rites performed by the Incas on the day of *Raymi*.[29] He kneels quite close to my bed and spends

---

[29]*Raymi*, principal feast of the Sun: the Inca and the priests worshipped him from a kneeling position.

considerable time in that uncomfortable position. Sometimes he falls silent and, eyes lowered, seems to be lost in a profound reverie. I see on his face that respectful consternation inspired in us when *the great Name*[30] is said aloud. If he finds an opportunity to seize my hand, he applies his mouth to it with the same veneration we show for the sacred diadem.[31] Sometimes he utters a great number of words that bear no resemblance to his nation's ordinary language. The sound is milder, more distinct, more measured. To these he adds the look of being profoundly moved that precedes tears, the kind of sighs that express the needs of the soul, intonings that are practically moans, indeed everything that accompanies the desire to obtain grace. Alas, dearest Aza, if he knew me well, if he were not somehow misinformed as to my being, what prayer would he have to make me?

Might not this nation be in some respect idolatrous? To this point I have seen no worship of the Sun. Perhaps women serve as the object of their devotion. Before the Great *Manco-Capac*[32] had brought the Sun's will to the earth, our ancestors sanctified all that struck fear or plea-

---

[30]The great Name was *Pachacamac*. It was uttered but rarely and with many signs of adoration.

[31]One kissed the diadem of *Manco-Capac* just as we kiss the relics of our saints.

[32]First lawgiver of the Indians. See *Histoire des Incas* [Garcilaso, *Royal Commentaries* 45–46; see translator's note on p. 14 and bracketed material in note 9].

sure in them. Perhaps these savages have those two feelings only for women.

But if they worshipped me, would they add to my misfortunes the wretched constraint they have imposed upon me? No, they would seek to please me and would obey the signs of my will. I would be free and would leave this hateful lodging. I would go seek out my soul's master. One look from him would erase the memory of so many misfortunes.

VI

What a horrible surprise, dearest Aza! How our misfortunes have been increased! How we are to be pitied! Our woes are without remedy: I have only to tell you of this and die.

They finally permitted me to arise from my bed, and I hastened to take advantage of this freedom. I dragged myself over to a small window, long the object of my inquisitive desires, and hurriedly opened it. But what did I see? Dear love of my life, I can find no expression to depict for you the extent of my shock and the mortal despair that gripped me upon finding there to be nothing about me save that terrible element the mere sight of which makes one tremble with fear.

My first glance explained only too well our dwelling's uncomfortable motion. I am in one of those floating houses of which the Spaniards made use to reach our unfortunate lands and of which I had been given only a highly imperfect description.

Can you imagine, dear Aza, what dire thoughts entered my soul along with this dreadful knowledge? I am certain that I am being taken away from you. I no longer breathe the same air or live in the same element that you do. You will never know where I am, whether I love you, whether I exist. The destruction of my being will not even seem a considerable enough event to be reported to you. Dear arbiter of my days, what value can my unfortunate life have for you from now on? Permit me to return to the Divinity an intolerable blessing that I no longer wish to enjoy; I shall never see you again, I no longer wish to live.

I am losing that which I love, and the universe is destroyed for me. It is nothing more than a vast desert that I fill with the cries of my love. Hear them, dear object of my tenderness, be moved by them, allow me to die . . .

What error is leading me astray! No, dearest Aza, no, it is not you who orders me to live, it is timid nature that, trembling with horror, has borrowed your voice, more powerful than its own, to defer an end it finds ever frightful. But now all is done with, and the most readily available means will deliver me from nature's regrets . . .

May the sea forever conceal in its depths my ill-fated tenderness, my life, and my despair.

Oh most unfortunate Aza, welcome my heart's last sentiments. It welcomed only your image, it wished to live only for you, it dies full of your love. I love you, I think it, I feel it still, I say it for the last time . . .

VII

Aza, you have not lost all. You still reign over a heart, for I breathe. The vigilance of my guards prevented the execution of my fatal plan, and I am left only with the shame of having attempted to carry it out. I will tell you nothing of the circumstances surrounding an intention thwarted the moment it was formed. Would I ever dare lift my eyes to look upon you had you borne witness to my fit of passion?

My reason, obliterated by despair, was no longer of any help to me. My life appeared of no value to me. I had forgotten your love.

How cruel is calm reflection after an outburst of madness! How different is one's perspective on the same objects! Gripped by the horror of despair, one takes savagery for courage and fear of suffering for resoluteness. Should a word, a glance, a surprise bring us back to ourselves, we find only weakness as the principle behind our heroism, repentance the only fruit of our labors, and scorn the only reward.

Knowing of my offense is its own harshest punishment. Abandoned to the bitterness of remorse, shrouded beneath a veil of shame, I hold myself aside, fearing lest my body take up too much space: I wish I could conceal it from the light. My tears flow in abundance, my sorrow is calm, no sound gives it expression, but I am entirely in its possession. Can I atone too much for my crime? It was against you.

For the past two days now, those beneficent savages have been trying in vain to make me share in the joy that thrills them. I can only guess at its cause, but even were it better known to me, I would not find myself worthy to join in their celebration. Their dances, their shouts of joy, a red liquor similar to maïs[33] that they drink in abundance, and their haste to gaze upon the Sun from every place whence they can see it would not have left me doubting that this rejoicing was in honor of the divine star were the conduct of the *Cacique* in accordance with that of the others.

But since the committing of my offense, far from taking part in the general celebration, he has shared only in my sorrow. His zeal is more respectful, his care more steadfast, his attention more insightful.

Grown aware that the continual presence of the savages belonging to his retinue added inhibition to my

---

[33]*Maïs* is a plant from which the Indians make a strong and healthful drink; they make offerings of it to the Sun on the days of his feasts, and they drink it to the point of inebriation after making the sacrifice. See *Hist. des Incas*, t. 2, p. 151 [Garcilaso, *Royal Commentaries* 86; see translator's note on p. 14 and bracketed material in note 9].

afflictions, he has delivered me from their importunate gazes, and I now have hardly any to tolerate save his own.

Would you believe it, dearest Aza? There are moments when I find there to be something pleasurable in this silent interaction. The fire of his eyes recalls the image of that fire I saw in yours, and the similarities I find in them seduce my heart. Alas, how fleeting that illusion is, and how lasting are the regrets that follow it! They will end only with the end of my life, since I live only for you.

VIII

When one single object draws all our thoughts, dearest Aza, events only interest us through the relations we find them to have with that object. If you were not my soul's only motive force, would I have gone, as I just now have, from the horror of despair to the sweetest hope? The *Cacique* had already tried several times without success to draw me to that window at which I can no longer look without trembling. Finally, pressed by new urgings, I allowed myself to be led to it. Oh my dear Aza, how richly was my accommodation rewarded!

By means of an unfathomable wonder, he let me see land from a distance at which, without the aid of this marvelous machine, a kind of hollowed out stick through which he had me look, the sight of my eyes would not have been able to reach it.

At the same time, he gave me to understand by means of signs which are growing familiar to me, that we are headed for that land and that the sight of it was the sole object of the rejoicing I had taken for a sacrifice to the Sun.

I sensed from the very first the full benefit of this discovery, and hope, like a ray of light, shone down to the very bottom of my heart.

Certainly I am being conducted to this land I have been made to see. Obviously it is part of your dominion since the Sun sheds its beneficent rays upon it.[34] I am no longer held by the bonds of those cruel Spaniards. Who then could prevent me from returning to being under your laws?

Yes, dear Aza, I am going to reunite myself with that which I love. Everything—my love, my reason, my desires—assures me that this is so. I fly into your arms, a flood of joy inundates my soul, the past fades away, my misfortunes are at an end, forgotten. I am occupied only with the future, it is my sole possession.

Aza, my dear hope, I have not lost you, I shall see your face, your clothes, your shadow. I shall love you, I shall tell it to you yourself. Are there any torments that such good fortune does not erase?

---

[34]The Indians did not know of our hemisphere and believed that the Sun only illuminated the land of its children.

IX

How long are the days when one is counting them, dearest Aza! Time like space is known only by its limits. Our ideas and our sight are equally lost when confronted with the constant uniformity of one or the other. If objects mark the boundaries of space, it seems to me that our hopes mark those of time and that if those hopes abandon us or cease to be clearly delineated, we no more perceive the duration of time than we do the air that fills all space.

Ever since the fatal instant of our separation, my soul and my heart, equally withered by misfortune, remained buried in a state of total neglect that is an abomination of nature and an image of nothingness. Days passed without my paying them any heed; no hope kept my attention fixed on their length. Now that hope marks every instant, their duration appears infinite to me, and in regaining my peace of mind, I taste the pleasure of regaining the ability to think.

Since my imagination has been opened to joy, a host of thoughts that come to it keep it busy to the point of tiring it out. Plans for pleasure and happiness alternate within it. New ideas are welcomed there with ease, and even those of which I was completely unaware engrave themselves upon it without my making any effort.

For two days now I have been able to understand several words in the *Cacique*'s language, which I did not think I knew. They are still only the names of objects and neither express my thoughts nor allow me to understand the thoughts of others; however, they have already provided me with several needed clarifications.

I know that the *Cacique*'s name is *Déterville*, that the floating house's is *vessel*, and that the land to which we are headed is called *France*.

At first that last one frightened me, for I do not recall having heard any part of your realm so named. But when I reflected upon the countless lands that are contained in it and whose names have escaped me, this first impulse toward fear soon vanished. Could it have survived for long in the company of the sturdy confidence ceaselessly given me by the sight of the Sun? No, dearest Aza, that divine star shines only upon its children; mere doubt would make me criminal. I am about to return to being under your rule; I have almost reached the moment of seeing you; I am racing toward my happiness.

Amid the transports of my joy, gratitude is preparing a delightful pleasure for me: you will shower the kindly *Cacique*[35] who is reuniting us with honors and riches. He will take the memory of Zilia with him to his province; having his virtue rewarded will make him yet more virtuous, and his good fortune will be to your glory.

———————————

[35]*Caciques* administered the Incas' tributary provinces.

Nothing, dearest Aza, can compare to the kindness he shows me. Far from treating me as his slave, he would seem to be mine, and I now experience as many marks of his efforts to please me as I did privations during my illness. Preoccupied with me, my worries, and my entertainment, he seems not to have any other cares. I receive his attentions with a bit less consternation now that, enlightened by habit and reflection, I see that I was mistaken about the idolatry of which I suspected him.

Not that he does not often repeat more or less the same actions that I took for signs of worship. But the tone, the expression, and the form that he employs in making them convince me that this behavior is a mere amusement in common use among those of his nation.

He starts by having me clearly pronounce some of the words of his language. As soon as I have repeated after him "Yes, I love you" or "I promise to be yours," joy spreads over his face and he kisses my hands with an excitement and look of good cheer altogether contrary to the seriousness that accompanies divine worship.

Now reassured in regard to his religion, I am not entirely so with respect to the country from which he hails. His language and his clothes are so different from ours that often my confidence is shaken. Upsetting reflections at times cloud my fondest hopes. I pass in turn from fear to joy and from joy to worry.

Fatigued by my mind's confusion, disheartened by the uncertainties that are tearing me apart, I had resolved not to think anymore, but how is one to slow the movement of a soul deprived of all communication that is acting only upon itself and is spurred to reflection by such strong interests? I am incapable of it, dearest Aza; I seek enlightenment with an urgency that consumes me, yet I continually find myself in the deepest darkness. I knew that being deprived of one sense can mislead in several respects, but I am surprised to see that the use of mine ushers me from one error to the next. Would the comprehension of languages also be that of the soul? Oh dear Aza! How my misfortunes make me glimpse upsetting truths! But let these sad thoughts leave me, for we are reaching land. The light of my days will dispel in a moment the shadows that surround me.

X

I have finally reached this land that had been the object of my desires, dearest Aza, but I have not yet seen anything here that presages the happiness I had been expecting. Everything that is offered to my eyes strikes, surprises, and astonishes me, leaving me with only a vague impression and a dumbfounded sense of confusion from which I do not even seek to deliver myself. My mistakes stifle my judgment, and I remain unsure, practically doubting even what I see.

Scarcely had we left the floating house when we entered a city built upon the seaside. The people who swarmed after us looked to me to be of the same nation as the *Cacique*, but the houses bear no resemblance to those in the cities of the Sun. If those cities possess houses of greater beauty thanks to the richness of their decoration, these are superior by virtue of the many marvels with which they are filled.

As I entered the room Déterville has made my lodging, my heart trembled, for in one of the corners I saw a young person dressed in the manner of a Virgin of the Sun. I ran to her with open arms. What a surprise, dearest Aza, what a great surprise it was to find nothing but an impenetrable resistance there where I saw a human figure moving about in a most extensive space!

My amazement held me transfixed, eyes locked onto that shadow, when Déterville drew my attention to his own figure next to the one with which I was completely preoccupied. I touched him, I spoke to him, and I saw him at once very near and very far from me.

These marvels disturb the mind and offend reason. What is one to think of this country's inhabitants? Must one fear them? Must one love them? I shall be careful to reserve judgment in this matter.

The *Cacique* gave me to understand that the figure I saw was my own, but what does that tell me? Is the marvel any less great? Am I any less mortified at finding only error and ignorance in my mind? I observe with sorrow, dearest Aza, that the least clever inhabitants of this Region are more learned than all our *Amautas*.

The *Cacique* has given me a most lively young *China*,[36] and it is indeed a great comfort to me again to see women and be served by them. Several others hasten to attend to my needs, which I would rather they not do as their presence awakens my fears. From the way they look at me, I see clearly that they have never been to *Cuzco*.[37] For the moment I am still unable to reach any firm conclusions: my spirit continues to float on a sea of uncertainties, my lonely, unwavering heart desires, expects, and awaits only a happiness without which all can be nothing but hardship.

XI

Although I have taken care to do everything in my power to shed some light on my situation, dearest Aza, I am no better informed of it than I was three days ago. I have been able to observe only that the savages of this region seem to be as good and humane as the *Cacique*: they sing and dance as if they had fields to plow every day.[38] If, to understand my current circumstances, I relied primarily

---

[36]Servant girl or chambermaid.
[37]Capital of Peru.
[38]Land was tended communally in Peru, and the days devoted to this work were days of celebration.

on the differences between their customs and those of our nation, I would lose all hope. But I recall that your august father subjugated quite distant provinces whose peoples bore no more relation to ours than do these: why should this not be one of them? The Sun, purer and more beautiful than I have ever seen, seems pleased to illuminate this land, and I am pleased to give myself over to the confidence he inspires in me. My only remaining worry concerns how much time will have to pass before I will be able to enlighten myself regarding our interests, for I am now convinced, dearest Aza, that use of the language of the land alone will inform me of the truth and bring my worries to an end.

I allow no opportunity to learn it slip away and avail myself of all moments when Déterville lets me do what I will to take lessons from my *China*. This is a feeble resource for, not being able to make her understand my thoughts, I cannot reason with her. At times the *Cacique's* signs are more useful to me. Habit has made of them a kind of language for us that at least serves us as a way to express our wishes. Yesterday he took me to a house where, without this mutual understanding, I would have conducted myself quite badly.

We entered a chamber much larger and more ornate than the one in which I live. Many people had gathered there. I was displeased by the general amazement shown at the sight of me. The excessive laughter that several young girls attempted to keep back and that started again when they looked upon me stirred in my heart a feeling so disturbing that I would have taken it for shame had I felt myself guilty of some offense. Finding only great repugnance at the thought of remaining with them, however, I was about to retrace my steps when a sign from Déterville held me back.

I understood that I would be committing an offense if I left and was quite careful to do nothing worthy of the blame being assigned me without cause; accordingly, I stayed and, focusing all my attention on those women, thought myself to have discerned that the singularity of my clothes alone caused the surprise of some and the offensive laughter of others. I felt pity for their weakness and from then on thought only of convincing them by my bearing that my soul did not differ so much from theirs as my clothing did from their finery.

A man whom I would have taken for a *Curacas*[39] had he not been dressed in black, came and took my hand in an affable manner, then led me over to a woman whose proud air made me take her for the region's *Pallas*.[40] He uttered several words that I know from having heard Déterville say them a thousand times: "How beautiful she is! What lovely eyes! . . ." Another man replied,

---

[39]*Curacas* were minor regional sovereigns one of whose privileges was wearing the same attire as the Incas.

[40]Generic term for princesses.

"What grace! The figure of a nymph! . . ." Apart from the women, who said nothing, everyone kept repeating more or less the same words. I do not know their meaning yet, but they surely convey pleasant ideas, for their utterance is always accompanied by a beaming coutenance.

The *Cacique* appeared extremely satisfied with what was being said. He remained forever at my side, or, if he moved off to speak with someone, his eyes never lost sight of me, and his signs advised me of what I should do. For my part, I was quite careful to observe him so as not to insult the customs of a nation so little aware of our own.

I know not, dearest Aza, if I will be able to make you understand how extraordinary these savages' manners appeared to me.

They are full of such an impatient liveliness that words do not satisfy their desire to express themselves, so they speak as much through the movements of their bodies as by the sounds of their voices. What I have seen of their ceaseless commotion has fully convinced me of the minor import of those displays by the *Cacique* that caused me such consternation and about which I entertained so many false conjectures.

Yesterday he kissed the hands of the *Pallas* as well as those of all the other women, even kissing them on the face. And there was another thing I had not seen before: men came up to him and embraced him as well. Some took him by the hand, others pulled at his clothing, and all of it with a swiftness of which we have absolutely no notion.

Judging their minds by the liveliness of their gestures, I am sure that our measured expressions and the sublime comparisons that so naturally express our tender feelings and affectionate thoughts would appear insipid to them. They would take our modest, serious demeanor for stupidity and the gravity of our gait for dullness. You will hardly believe it, dearest Aza, but despite their imperfections, if you were here, I would be quite content in their company. A certain air of affability infusing all that they do makes them likeable, and if my soul were happier, I would take pleasure from the variety of objects that are successively presented to my eyes. But the slight relation they have with you erases the charms of their novelty. You are my sole source of benefit and pleasures.

XII

I have gone quite some time, dearest Aza, without being able to devote a single moment to my favorite occupation; however, I have quite a number of extraordinary things to tell you. I shall take advantage of a bit of leisure to try to inform you of them.

The day after my visit to the home of the *Pallas*, Déterville had me brought a most beautiful garment of the customary sort in this country. After my little *China* had settled it upon me to her liking, she led me to that inge-

56

nious device that duplicates objects. Much as I should have grown accustomed to its effects, I could not help being surprised at seeing myself as if I were standing opposite myself.

My new attire did not displease me. Perhaps I would miss that which I am giving up more had it not caused me to be looked at everywhere with discomforting attention.

At the moment when the *Cacique* entered my room, the young maid was still adding a few trinkets to my finery. He stopped in the doorway and looked at us for some time without speaking. So profound was his reverie that he stepped aside to let the *China* pass and resumed his former position without realizing it. Eyes riveted upon me, he looked over my entire person with a serious attention that made me feel ill-at-ease without knowing the reason for this.

In the meantime, to demonstrate my appreciation for this new act of kindness, I held out my hand to him and, unable to express my sentiments, thought it impossible to say to him anything more pleasing than a few of those words he so enjoyed having me repeat. I even endeavored to give them the tone he gives them.

I do not know what effect they had on him at that particular moment, but his eyes grew bright, his face turned crimson, he approached me with a troubled look and appeared to want to take me in his arms. Then, suddenly stopping, he firmly shook my hand and said in an emotional voice, "No . . . respect . . . her virtue . . ." along with several other words that I understand no better, then raced to the other end of the room and threw himself into his chair where he remained with his head in his hands showing all the signs of deep sorrow.

I was alarmed at his condition, not doubting that I had caused him some pain. I went to him to demonstrate my repentance, but he gently pushed me away without looking at me, and I dared not say anything more to him. I was in a state of the greatest consternation, when the domestics entered to bring us food. He arose and we ate together in the accustomed manner, a hint of sadness the only apparent consequence of his sorrow, for he showed me no less kindness and consideration than before. This all seems unfathomable to me.

I did not dare lift my eyes to look upon him or use the signs that normally took the place of conversation between us. We were eating at a time so different from the normal hour of our meals, however, that I could not help making known to him my surprise. All I understood from his response was that we were going to change dwellings. Indeed, after coming and going several times, the *Cacique* finally came and took me by the hand. I allowed myself to be led, musing all the while on what had happened and trying to determine if this change of place might not be some sort of consequence of it.

Scarcely had we passed through the final door of the house when he helped me climb a rather high step, and I found myself in a little room. One cannot stand up in it without inconvenience, and there is not enough room to walk about, but the *Cacique*, the *China*, and I were able to seat ourselves there most comfortably. This little place is pleasantly furnished, and windows on either side light it adequately.

Oh dearest Aza, how common are marvels in this land, for while I was looking upon Déterville with surprise and trying to imagine why he had placed us in such close quarters, I felt that machine or cabin—I know not what to call it—move and change position! This movement made me think of the floating house, and I was gripped with fear, but the *Cacique*, attentive to my slightest worries, put my mind at ease by having me see through one of the windows that this machine, hanging fairly close to the ground, moved by means of a secret I did not understand.

Déterville then drew my attention to several *Hamas*[41] of a kind completely unknown to us walking in front of this machine and dragging us along. One must, oh light of my days, have superhuman genius to invent such useful and distinctive things. But this nation must also

_____

[41]Generic name for animals.

have a few great faults that curb its power since it is not mistress of the entire world.

For four days now we have been shut inside this marvelous device, only leaving it at night to rest in the first dwelling we find, and I never leave it without regret. I must admit to you, dearest Aza, that despite my tender worries, I have savored pleasures during this journey that were unknown to me. Enclosed in the temple from tenderest childhood, I was not acquainted with the beauties of the universe. What a good thing I had been missing!

Oh friend of my heart, it must be that nature endowed its works with an unknown appeal that even the most skilled art cannot imitate. What I have seen of the wonders invented by men has not caused me anything like the rapture I feel when admiring the universe. The vast countrysides that are forever changing and being renewed before my eyes transport my soul just as quickly as we cross them.

The eyes at once glance over, embrace, and rest upon an infinite number of objects as varied as they are pleasing. One thinks that the only limits to one's sight to be found are the ends of the world itself. This error flatters us, for it gives us a satisfying notion of our own stature and seems to bring us closer to the Creator of so many marvels.

At the end of a beautiful day, the sky offers images whose pomp and magnificence greatly surpass those of the earth.

On the one hand, transparent clouds gathered about the setting sun offer our eyes mountains of shadow and light whose majestic disorder draw our wonder to the point of forgetting ourselves; on the other, a less brilliant star rises, receiving and spreading a less vivid light on objects that, losing their activity in the absence of the Sun, now strike our senses in a manner that is but sweet, peaceful, and in perfect harmony with the silence reigning upon the earth. Then, as we return to our senses, a delicious calm penetrates our souls, and we delight in the universe as if possessing it alone, for we see nothing in it that does not belong to us. A sweet serenity leads us to pleasant reflections, and if a few regrets come to disturb *education, think for herself* them, they are born only of the necessity to tear ourselves from this sweet reverie to enclose ourselves once again in the mad prisons that men have made for themselves and that all their ingenuity will never be able to render anything more than contemptible when compared to the works of nature.

The *Cacique* was kind enough to help me out of the rolling cabin every day to let me gaze at leisure upon that which he saw me admiring with such satisfaction.

While the beauties of the heavens and the earth exert such a powerful attraction on our souls, the simpler, more touching beauties of the forest caused me neither less pleasure nor less amazement.

How delightful are the woods, dearest Aza! As one enters, a universal charm spreads over all the senses and blurs their roles. One thinks oneself to be seeing the coolness before feeling it; the different shadings of the colors of the leaves soften the light that penetrates them and seem to strike the emotions as soon as they strike the eye. A pleasant yet indeterminate odor barely allows one to discern whether it is being tasted or smelled; and the very air, unnoticed, conveys to our entire being a pure, sensual delight that seems to give us an additional sense even if we cannot name its organ.

Oh my dear Aza, how your presence would make such pure pleasures lovelier still! How I wished to be sharing them with you! As witness to my tenderest thoughts, I would have made you find in the sentiments of my heart charms yet more moving than those of the beauty of the universe.

XIII

Here I am, dearest Aza, in a city named Paris. Our journey has come to an end, but by all appearances, my troubles have not.

More attentive than ever since my arrival here to all that is going on, I have made discoveries that cause me nothing but torment and bode only unhappiness. I find the thought of you in the least of my inquisitive desires yet encounter it in none of the objects offering themselves to my view.

As best I can judge from the time it took us to cross this city and the great number of inhabitants filling the streets, it contains more people than could be assembled in two or three of our provinces.

I recall the wondrous things I was told of *Quitu* and seek to find here a few features in common with the way that great city was portrayed to me. But alas, what a difference!

This one contains bridges, rivers, trees, farmland; it seems more like an entire universe than a single dwelling place. In vain would I attempt to give you an accurate idea of the height of the houses, for they are so prodigiously elevated that it is easier to believe that nature produced them as they are than to understand how men could have built them.

It is here that the family of the *Cacique* makes its home. The house in which they dwell is almost as magnificent as the Sun's. The furnishings and a few sections of the walls are made of gold. The rest of the walls are covered with a multihued material consisting of the most beautiful colors that depict the beauties of nature reasonably well.

When we arrived, Déterville gave me to understand that he was taking me to his mother's room. We found her in a semireclined position on a bed of roughly the same form as those of the *Incas* and made of the same metal.[42] After presenting her hand to the *Cacique*, who kissed it while bowing so deeply that he practically scraped the ground, she embraced him, but with such cold kindness and restrained joy that, had I not been told, I never would have recognized the sentiments of nature in that mother's caress.

After they had conversed for a moment, the *Cacique* had me approach. She threw me a scornful glance and, without replying to what her son was telling her, gravely continued winding about her fingers a length of cord hanging from a little piece of gold.

Déterville left us to go up to a tall man of healthy appearance who had taken a few steps toward him. He embraced this man as well as another woman engaged in the same occupation as the *Pallas*.

The moment the *Cacique* had appeared in that room, a young girl of roughly my age had rushed in. She followed him with a timid urgency that was most remarkable. Joy shone upon her face without banishing from it an intriguing bit of underlying sadness. Déterville embraced her last but with such natural tenderness that my heart was moved by it. Alas, dearest Aza, how great would be our transports if, after so many misfortunes, fate were to reunite us!

---

[42]The Incas' beds, chairs, and tables were solid gold.

During this time, I remained near the *Pallas*, out of respect;[43] I dared not move away from her or lift my eyes to meet her gaze. A few harsh glances that she cast upon me from time to time served to intimidate me completely and caused me an embarrassment that inhibited my very thoughts.

Finally, as if the young girl had guessed my consternation, she left Déterville, took me by the hand, and led me to a window near which we sat down. Although I understood nothing of what she was telling me, her eyes, filled as they were with goodness, spoke to me in the universal language of kind hearts and inspired trust and friendliness in me. I would have liked to reveal my feelings to her, but being unable to express myself according to my wishes, I said aloud all that I knew of her language.

She smiled at this more than once while looking at Déterville in a fine and gentle fashion. I was taking pleasure from this form of conversation when the *Pallas* looked at the young girl and spoke a few rather loud words to her. She lowered her eyes, pushed away my hand, which she had been holding in hers, and looked at me no more.

Some time after that, an old woman with harsh features entered the room, approached the *Pallas*, then walked over to me, took me by the arm, and led me practically against

---

[43]Even girls of royal blood harbored great respect for married women.

my will to a room in the highest part of the house, where she left me alone.

Although that moment must not have been my life's unhappiest, it was not, dearest Aza, one of its least annoying either. I was expecting the end of my journey to bring some kind of relief to my worries and was counting on at least finding amid the *Cacique*'s family the same marks of kindness he had shown me. The cool welcome of the *Pallas*, the sudden change in the young girl's manner, the abruptness of that woman who had torn me from a place where I had an interest in staying, the inattentiveness of Déterville, who in no way opposed the form of violence inflicted upon me—indeed, all the circumstances that an unhappy soul can find to augment its sufferings presented themselves to me at once in their saddest light. I believed myself to have been abandoned by everyone and was bitterly lamenting my dreadful fate when I saw my *China* come in. On account of the state I was in, the sight of her struck me as a stroke of good fortune. I ran to her and embraced her as my tears flowed. She was touched by this, and her display of emotion was precious to me, for when one thinks oneself to have been reduced to feeling sorry for oneself, the sympathy of others is valued quite highly. That girl's marks of affection eased my pain. I told her my troubles as if she could understand me. I asked her a thousand questions as if she could answer them. Her tears spoke to my heart, mine continued to flow, but they now contained less bitterness.

I still hoped to see Déterville at mealtime, but I was served my food, and I saw no sign of him. Since losing you, dear idol of my heart, this *Cacique* is the only human being who has shown me kindness without interruption. The habit of seeing him has turned into a need, and his absence redoubled my sadness. After waiting for him in vain, I went to bed, but sleep had in no way dried my tears when I saw him enter my room followed by the young person whose sudden scorn had struck me such a sensitive blow.

She threw herself upon my bed and, through a thousand caresses, seemed to wish to make amends for her earlier ill treatment of me.

The *Cacique* sat next to the bed. He seemed to take as much pleasure from seeing me as I felt at not having in any way been abandoned. They looked at me as they conversed and overwhelmed me with a stream of the tenderest marks of affection.

This conversation imperceptibly grew more serious. Without understanding their words, I was easily able to determine that they were based on trust and friendship. I was very careful not to interrupt them, but as soon as they came back to me, I endeavored to draw from the *Cacique* clarification of that which had struck me as most extraordinary since my arrival.

All that I could understand from his replies was that the young girl I saw before me was named Céline and that she was his sister, that the tall man I had seen in the *Pallas*'s room was his older brother, and that the other young woman was this brother's wife.

Céline became more precious to me when I learned that she was the *Cacique*'s sister. They both provided me with such pleasant company that I was utterly unaware of day's having dawned before they left me.

After their departure, I spent the rest of the time intended for repose conversing with you; this is my only possession, my only source of joy. It is to you alone, dear soul of my thoughts, that I reveal my heart. You will ever be the sole guardian of my secrets, my tenderness, and my feelings.

XIV

Dearest Aza, were I not to continue to take the time I devote to you from the time I sleep, I would no longer enjoy these delicious moments when I exist only for you. I have been made again to don my Virgin's attire and am obliged to spend the entire day in a room filled with a crowd of people that is forever changing and being renewed and that scarcely ever diminishes.

This unsought dissipation often tears me in spite of myself from my tender thoughts. But if for a few instants I lose that rapt attention ceaselessly joining my soul to yours, I soon find you again in the favorable comparisons I make between you and all that surrounds me.

In the various regions I have traveled, I have seen no other savages so haughtily familiar as these. The women especially seem to me to have a scornful kindness that flies in the face of human decency and that might well inspire in me as much scorn for them as they show for others were I to know them better.

One of them caused me an affront yesterday that still distresses me today. At a time when the number of those present was greatest, she had already spoken to several people without noticing me. Whether by chance or because someone had pointed me out to her, she glanced in my direction, burst out laughing, then hastily moved from where she had been standing to approach me, had me stand up, and, after turning me around and around as many times as her high spirits moved her to and touching all parts of my attire with scrupulous attention, she beckoned over a young man and recommended with him this examination of my person.

Although I found repugnant the liberties both of them were taking, the sumptuousness of the woman's dress made me assume her to be a *Pallas*, and the splendor of the young man's, all covered with patches of gold, to assume him to be an *Anqui*,[44] so I dared not oppose their

***

[44]Prince of the blood: wearing gold on one's clothing required the Inca's permission, and he only granted it to princes of royal blood.

will. But when that rash savage, made bold by the familiarity of the *Pallas* and perhaps by my reserve, had the
audacity to put his hand on my breast, I pushed him away
with a surprise and indignation that let him know I was
better schooled than he in the rules of civilized behavior.

Hearing my cry, Déterville ran over. No sooner had
the *Cacique* said a few words to him than the young
savage leaned on his shoulder and issued laughter so violent that it contorted his face.

Déterville pushed the young man's hand from his
shoulder and spoke to him, face flushed, in a tone so cold
that the young man's hilarity vanished. Apparently having
nothing more to say in reply, the young man moved off
without making answer and came around no more.

Oh my dearest Aza! How the manners in these coun-
tries fill me with respect for those of the children of the
Sun! How the rashness of that young *Anqui* recalls to my
mind the dear memory of your tender respect, your
modest reserve, and the charms of the courtesy prevail-
ing over our relations! I felt it the first moment I caught
sight of you, dear delight of my soul, and I will feel it all
my life. You alone combine all the perfections that
nature has scattered separately among other humans,
just as nature has assembled in my heart all those feelings of tenderness and admiration that link me to you
until death.

XV

The longer I live with the *Cacique* and his sister, dearest Aza, the harder I find it to convince myself that they are of this nation; they alone know and respect virtue.

Céline's simple manners, childlike kindness, and modest good cheer would readily make one think she had been brought up among our Virgins. The sweet decency and tender seriousness of her brother would easily persuade one that he is born of the blood of *Incas*. They both treat me in as humane a fashion as would we them if misfortunes had brought them to us. I no longer even doubt that the *Cacique* is one of your tributaries.[45]

He never enters my room without making a gift to me of a few of those marvels in which this region abounds. Sometimes he gives me bits of that machine that duplicates objects, enclosed in little cases made of wondrous material. Other times I receive light and surprisingly brilliant stones with which they decorate practically all parts of the body here, for these stones are affixed to the ears, worn on the stomach, at the throat, on shoes, and the result is very pleasing to see.

But what I find most entertaining is a kind of small tool they make from a very hard metal that is of singular

---

[45]*Caciques* and *Curacas* were obliged to provide the *Inca* and the queen their clothing and supplies. They never appeared before these two without offering them as tribute a sampling of the curiosities produced by the province under their command.

usefulness. Some serve to create works that Céline is teaching me to make. Others of a cutting shape serve to divide up all sorts of fabrics from which one can make as many pieces as one likes, without strain, and in a way that is most amusing.

I have come across countless other rarities yet more extraordinary, but because they are in no way part of our customs, I find no terms in our language capable of giving you an idea of them.

I am carefully preserving all these offerings for you, dearest Aza, for in addition to the pleasure I will obtain from your surprise when you see them, they are most assuredly yours. Were the *Cacique* not your obedient subject, would he pay me a tribute that he knows to be due only on account of your supreme rank? The respects he has always paid me have led me to believe that my birth is known to him. The presents with which he honors me convince me beyond any doubt that he is not unaware that I am to be your spouse, for he treats me in advance as he would a *Mama-Oella*.[46]

This conviction reassures me and calms some portion of my worries. I understand that I lack only freedom of expression to learn from the *Cacique* the reasons that compel him to detain me in his home and to convince

----

[46]Name taken by the queen upon ascending to the throne.

him to remand me to your power. Until then, however, I shall still have many more pains to suffer.

The temperament of *Madame*—that is the name of Déterville's mother—is not nearly as friendly as that of her children. Far from treating me with as much kindness, on all occasions she bears me a mortifying coldness and disdain whose cause I am unable to discover. Furthermore, by virtue of a contradiction of sentiment I understand still less, she requires that I continually be with her.

For me, this is an intolerable discomfort. Constraint prevails wherever she is, and it is only on the sly that Céline and her brother make me signs of their friendship. They themselves dare not speak freely in front of her and therefore continue to spend part of their nights in my room, for it is the only time when we can enjoy in peace the pleasure of seeing one another, and although I hardly participate in their discussions, I always find their presence agreeable. It stems not from the care the two of them provide that I am not happy. Alas, dearest Aza, they are unaware that happiness is impossible for me when I am far from you, and that I only believe myself to be living to the extent that your memory and my tenderness occupy me entirely.

XVI

I have so few *quipus* left, dearest Aza, that I scarcely dare use them. When I wish to knot them, the fear of seeing them run out stops me, as if by saving them I could multiply their number. I am going to lose my soul's pleasure, my life's support. Nothing will ease the weight of your absence, and I shall be overwhelmed by it.

I tasted of an exquisite delight in preserving the memory of my heart's most secret transports in order to offer them to you in homage. I wished to preserve the memory of this singular nation's principal customs to bring amusement to your moments of leisure in happier days. Alas, I have but little hope left of being able to carry out my plans.

If at present I find it so difficult to organize my thoughts, how could I subsequently recall them without some form of outside help? One form is being offered me, but making use of it is so difficult that I believe this to be impossible.

The *Cacique* has brought me a Savage of this Region who comes every day to give me lessons in his language and in the method used here to give a kind of existence to thoughts. This is done by drawing with a feather little figures called *letters* on a thin, white material they call *paper*. These figures have names, and those names, when mixed together, stand for the sounds of the words. But those names and those sounds seem so little different one from another that if I succeed in understanding them one day, I am quite confident it will not be without great effort. That poor savage goes to unbelievably great lengths to teach me, I go to even greater lengths to learn, and yet I make so little progress that I would give up the undertaking if I knew that another path could enlighten me about your fate and mine.

But there is no other, dearest Aza! Accordingly, henceforth I will take pleasure only in this new and singular study. I would like to live alone so as to apply myself to it without interruption, and the obligation imposed upon me to be forever in *Madame*'s room is becoming torture for me.

In the beginning, by arousing the curiosity of others, I amused my own, but when only the eyes can be used, they are soon sated. All the women paint their faces the same color. They always adopt the same manner, and I believe that they always say the same things. Appearances are more varied among the men. A few look as though they are thinking, but in general I suspect this nation of not being at all as it appears: affectation seems to me to be its dominant trait.

Were the shows of zeal and attentiveness with which they dress up the least social duties here natural, these peoples would have to have more goodness and humanity in their hearts than do ours. Is this conceivable, dearest Aza?

Had they as much serenity in their souls as on their faces, were the penchant for joy that I notice in all

their actions sincere, would they choose for their amusement spectacles such as the one I was made to see?

I was brought to a place where they act out, more or
less as in your palace, the deeds of men who are no
more,[47] but with this difference: while we evoke the
memory of only the wisest and most virtuous, I believe
that here they celebrate only those who were insane or
evil. Those who represent these personages shout and
flail about like madmen. I saw one of them push his fury
to the point of killing himself. Beautiful women, whom
they apparently torment, are forever crying and make
gestures of despair which have no need of the words that
accompany them to convey the great excess of these
women's pain.

Is it to be believed, dearest Aza, that an entire people
of such humane outward appearance takes pleasure in
the depiction of misfortunes and crimes that degraded
and burdened their fellows in days gone by?

But perhaps one has need here of the horror of vice to
lead one to virtue. That thought comes to me without
my seeking it, and if it were correct, how I would pity
this nation! Ours, more favored by nature, cherishes the
good on account of its own appeal. We have need only of
models of virtue to become virtuous, just as one need
only love you to become loveable.

---

[47]The Incas had performed a kind of drama whose subjects were
drawn from the best actions of their predecessors.

XVII

I no longer know what to think of this nation's true spirit, dearest Aza. It goes from one extreme to the other with such speed that one would have to be cleverer than I to establish a firm judgment as to its character.

I was made to see a spectacle completely the opposite of the first one. That cruel and terrifying display was revolting to the mind and humiliating to one's humanity, whereas this one was amusing and agreeable in its imitation of nature and homage to common sense. It consists of a much greater number of men and women than did the first. They also depict actions from human life in it, but whether they are expressing pain or pleasure, joy or sorrow, it is done through songs and dances.

It must be the case, dearest Aza, that the understanding of sounds is universal, for I had no more difficulty experiencing the emotion of the various passions being depicted than I would have had they been expressed in our language, and this seems quite natural to me.

Human language is no doubt of man's invention since it differs by nation. Nature, more powerful and more attentive to the needs and pleasures of its creatures, gave those creatures general means of expressing their desires, and those means are imitated very well by the songs I heard.

If it is true that piercing sounds better express the need for help in a state of violent fear or of acute pain than do words understood in one part of the world that have no meaning in the other, it is no less certain that tender moans instill a much more effective compassion in our hearts than do words whose strange arrangement often has the opposite effect.

Do not light, bright sounds inevitably bring merriment to our hearts that the telling of an amusing anecdote or clever joke never spawns but imperfectly?

Are there expressions in any language that can communicate naive pleasure with as much success as can the frolicking of animals? It seems that dances seek to imitate it or at the very least inspire approximately the same feeling.

Anyway, in this presentation, all is in conformity with nature and humanity. Oh dearest Aza, what deed can one do for men equal in goodness to that of inspiring joy in them?

I was feeling that joy myself and being thrilled by it practically in spite of myself, when it was clouded by an incident that befell Céline.

As we were leaving, we strayed a little from the rest of the crowd and were holding each other up for fear of falling. Déterville was a few steps ahead of us escorting his sister-in-law, when a young savage of friendly countenance approached Céline, murmured a few words to her, handed her a small piece of paper that she scarcely had the strength to accept, and moved off.

Céline, who had grown so frightened at his approach as to make me share the tremor that gripped her, turned her head languidly in his direction when he left us. She looked so weak to me that, thinking she had suddenly taken ill, I was going to call Déterville to her aid, but she stopped me, commanding my silence by putting one of her fingers over my mouth. I preferred continuing to worry to disobeying her.

That same night, when brother and sister joined me in my room, Céline showed the *Cacique* the paper she had received. Based on the little I could gather from their conversation, I would have thought she loved the young man who had given it to her, were it possible that one be frightened by the presence of that which one loves.

I could share with you yet more observations I have made, dearest Aza, but alas, I see the end of my cords drawing near. I am touching their last threads and tying their last knots. These knots, which seemed to me to be a line of communication linking my heart to yours, are already nothing more than the sad objects of my regret. Illusion is deserting me, replaced by the awful truth: my wandering thoughts, lost in the immense void of absence, will henceforth be reduced to nothing with the same speed as time. Dear Aza, I feel as if we were being separated yet again, that I am being torn from your love anew. Oh Aza, dear hope of my heart, I am losing you,

I am leaving you, I will see you no more! How far apart we are to be!

XVIII

How much time has been erased from my life! The Sun has made half its journey, dearest Aza, since the last time I enjoyed the artificial pleasure I created for myself by believing that I was conversing with you. How long this double absence has seemed for me! What courage has it not required of me to bear it? I lived only in the future, for the present no longer seemed worthy of being counted. All my thoughts were no more than desires, my reflections only plans, my feelings only hopes.

I am still barely able to form these figures that I rush to make the interpreters of my tenderness. ~~writing is~~ I feel myself being brought back to life by this tender ~~lifesaver~~ occupation. Restored to myself, I feel as if I am beginning *independence* to live again. Oh Aza, how dear you are to me, what joy I feel in telling you so, in depicting this fact, in giving this sentiment all the kinds of existence it can have! I would like to inscribe it on the hardest metal, on the walls of my room, on my clothes, on all that surrounds me, and express it in all languages.

Alas, how grievous has it been for me knowing the one I now use, how deceptive the hope that led me to learn it! As I gained understanding of it, a new universe presented itself to my eyes. Objects took another form, and each clarification revealed to me a new misfortune.

Everything—my mind, my heart, my eyes—everything led me astray. Even the Sun tricked me, for it illuminates the entire world, of which your domain occupies but a part, as do many other realms that make it up. Do not believe, dearest Aza, that I have been deceived in regard to these unbelievable facts, for they have been proven to me only too well.

Far from being among peoples subject to obey you, I find myself not only under foreign dominion but so far from your empire that our nation would still be unknown in these parts had not the greed of the Spaniards caused them to overcome horrific dangers to make their way to us.

Will not love accomplish what the thirst for riches has been able to? If you love me, if you desire me, if you still think of unfortunate Zilia, I should expect everything of your tenderness or your generosity. Should I be informed of the paths able to bring me to you, the dangers to be overcome and strains to be borne will be pleasures for my heart. *taken for granted - no longer certain that he (7's her.*

XIX

I am still so unskilled in the art of writing, dearest Aza, that it takes me an endless amount of time to form a very few lines. It often happens that after having written

81

a great deal, I myself cannot figure out what I believed myself to be expressing. This confusion clouds my thoughts and makes me forget what I had with difficulty recalled to my mind. I start over, I do no better, and yet I go on.

I would find greater ease in this if I had to depict for you only the forms taken by my tenderness, for then the vividness of my feelings would smooth away all difficulties. But I would also like to give you an account of all that has happened during the interval of my silence. I would like for you not to be unaware of any of my actions; nevertheless, for so long now they have held so little interest and been so like one to another that it would be impossible for me to distinguish them.

The most important event in my life has been Déterville's departure. *miss D. ways she missed*

For a span of time they call *six months*, he has been off making war on behalf of his sovereign's interests. When he left, I was still ignorant of the use of his language. From the sharp pain he manifested in taking leave of his sister and me, however, I understood that we were losing him for a long time.

I shed many tears over this fact, and my heart was filled with a thousand fears that Céline's kind attentions could not erase. I was losing in him my most solid hope of seeing you again. To whom could I have recourse if new misfortunes were to befall me? I was understood by no one.

I was not long in feeling the effects of this absence. *Madame*, whose scorn I had divined only too well, and who had kept me in her room so much of the time solely out of I know not what kind of vanity that she derived, I am told, from my birth and from the power she has over me, had me shut away with Céline in a house of Virgins, where we are still.

This retreat would not displease me were it not depriving me, at the moment when I am in a position to understand everything, of the information I need concerning the plan I am forming to go join you. The Virgins who inhabit this dwelling are of such profound ignorance that they are unable to satisfy my slightest curiosities.

The worship they offer their country's Divinity requires that they renounce all his blessings: knowledge of the mind, feelings of the heart, and I think even reason itself, or at least so their speech would lead one to believe.

Shut away like ours, these Virgins have one advantage that is not enjoyed in the temples of the Sun: here the walls are open in a few places where thay are covered only by crossed pieces of iron set close enough together to prevent one's leaving but which allow one to see and speak with people from outside. These places are called *parlors*.

It is thanks to this amenity that I continue to take writing lessons. I speak only with the master who gives them to me, and his ignorance of all matters save his art cannot remove me from my own. Céline does not seem to be any better informed, for I notice in her answers to my questions a certain consternation that can stem only from an awkward attempt at dissimulation or from a shameful level of ignorance. Whatever the case, her conversation is always limited to the concerns of her heart and those of her family.

As I suspected, the young Frenchman who spoke to her one day as she was leaving the spectacle where they sing is her suitor. But Madame Déterville, who does not want to marry them, forbids her to see him and, to be surer of preventing her from doing so, wants her not to speak to anyone whatsoever.

It is not that Céline's choice is unworthy of her; rather, it is that her vain and unnatural mother is taking advantage of a barbarous custom established among the great noblemen of this land to force Céline to don Virgin's garb so as to make her elder son richer. For this same reason, she has already forced Déterville to choose a certain religious order that he will never be able to leave once he has uttered certain words called *vows*.

Céline is resisting with all her might the sacrifice being required of her, and her courage is sustained by her suitor's letters, which I receive from my writing master and pass on to her. Her sorrow has brought such a change to her character, however, that far from showing me the same kindness she used to when I did not speak her language, she now infuses our relations with a bitterness that sharpens my pain.

Perpetual confidante for Céline's troubles, I listen to her without irritation, offer sympathy without effort, and console her with friendship. And if my tenderness, awakened by the depiction of her own, causes me to seek relief from my heart's oppression by merely uttering your name aloud, impatience and scorn grow visible on her face, and she disputes my claims regarding your mind, your virtues, your very love.

Even my *China* (I know of no other name for her, that one seemed pleasing, and so it has been left upon her), my *China* who seemed to like me and who obeys me on all other occasions, has the audacity to urge me not to think about you anymore. And if I order her to be silent, she leaves, Céline comes, and I must hold in my sorrow. This tyranical constraint brings my woes to their peak. All I have left is the sole and pathetic satisfaction of covering this paper with expressions of my tenderness, as it is the only compliant witness to my heart's sentiment.

Alas, the trouble to which I am going may well be useless! Perhaps you will never know that I lived only for you. This horrible thought weakens my courage without dissuading me from continuing to write you. I preserve my illusion to preserve my life for you, I set aside barbarous reason that would enlighten me, for if I were not to hope of seeing you again, I would perish, dearest Aza, of this I am certain; without you, living is torture for me.

XX

Until now, dearest Aza, I have been preoccupied with the pains of my heart and have told you nothing of those afflicting my mind, yet they are hardly less cruel. I feel one of a sort unknown among us that is caused by the general customs of this nation. These customs are so different from ours that unless I give you some idea of them, you will be unable to sympathize with my anxiety.

This empire's government, entirely unlike your own, cannot help but be deficient. Whereas the *Capa-Inca* is obliged to provide for the sustenance of his peoples, in Europe the sovereigns derive theirs solely from the work of their subjects; thus, nearly all crime and unhappiness arise from ill-satisfied needs.

The unhappiness of the nobles is generally born of the difficulties they encounter attempting to reconcile their apparent splendor with their actual misery.

Ordinary men can only maintain their state by means of what is called commerce or industry, and bad faith is the least of the crimes that result from it.

A part of the people is obliged to have recourse to the humanity of others just to live, and the results of their entreaties are so meager that these wretches barely have enough to keep from dying.

Without having gold, one cannot acquire a portion of this earth that nature has given to all men. Without possessing what is called property, one cannot have gold, and by a logical inconsistency that wounds the lights of natural intelligence and exasperates reason, this proud nation, in accordance with the laws of a false honor of its own invention, attaches shame to receiving from anyone other than the sovereign that which is necessary to sustain life and standing. This sovereign spreads his largesse over such a small number of his subjects in comparison with the quantity of the wretched that it would be just as mad to lay claim to a share of it as it would be ignominious to deliver oneself by death from the impossibility of living without shame.

 At first my acquaintance with these sad truths roused my heart only to pity for those wretches and indignation at the laws of this land. But alas, how the disdainful manner I heard used to speak of those who are not rich impelled me to make a few cruel reflections upon myself! I have neither gold nor land nor an occupation, yet I must be one of the citizens of this city. Oh heavens above, to what class am I to assign myself?

Much as any shame not deriving from the commission of an actual misdeed is alien to me and much as I sense how foolish it is to feel shame because of matters beyond my will and power, I cannot help suffering on account of the idea others have of me. This hardship would be unbearable to me were I not to hope that one day your generosity will put me in a position to compensate those who humiliate me in spite of myself through acts of kindness by which I thought myself to be honored.

Not that Céline does not do all she can to calm my fears in this regard, but what I see and learn of the people of this country leads me to be generally wary of their words. Their virtues, dearest Aza, have no more reality than their riches. The furniture I thought made of gold is only coated with that metal while truly being built of wood; likewise, what they call politeness thinly conceals their faults beneath the outward appearance of virtue. By paying a bit of attention, however, one can discover its artificial quality just as easily as one can that of their false riches.

I owe a part of this knowledge to a kind of writing called *books*. Although I still have great difficulty understanding their contents, they are most useful to me, and I learn basic notions from them. Céline explains to me what she knows of them, and I then form ideas I think to be correct.

Some of these books explain what men have done, others what they have thought. I cannot tell you, dearest Aza, the high degree of pleasure I would derive from reading them if I understood them better or the extreme desire I have to know some of the divine men who compose them. I realize that they are to the soul what the Sun is to the earth and that in their company I would find all the lights of learning and all the help I need. But I see no hope of ever having that satisfaction. Although Céline reads rather frequently, she is not learned enough to give me satisfaction, for she had barely given a thought to books' being created by men and does not know these men's names or even if they are still alive.

Dearest Aza, I shall bring you all that I can gather of these marvelous works, I shall explain them to you in our language, and I shall taste of the supreme happiness of providing a new pleasure to that which I love. Alas, will I ever be able to do so?

XXI

I shall no longer lack for material to discuss with you, dearest Aza, for I was made to speak with a *Cusipata*, called a *monk* here. A man knowledgeable about every-thing, he promised to leave me ignorant of nothing. Polite as a great nobleman and learned as an *Amauta*, he knows the ways of the world as well as he knows the dogmas of his religion. His conversation, more useful than a book, gave me a satisfaction of which I had not tasted since my misfortunes separated me from you.

He came to give me instruction in the religion of France and to urge me to embrace it.

From the manner in which he spoke to me of the vir-tues it prescribes, those virtues are drawn from natural law and are truly as pure as our own, but I do not have a subtle enough mind to perceive the relation supposed to exist between that religion and this nation's manners and customs. On the contrary, I find there to exist such a striking inconsistency between them that my reason absolutely refuses to subscribe to it.

As for the origins and principles of this religion, they did not seem to me to be any more unbelievable than the story of *Mancocapa* and swamp *Tisicaca*,[48] and its moral teachings are so beautiful that I would have listened to the *Cusipata* with a more accommodating attitude had he not spoken contemptuously of the sacred worship we offer the Sun, for any partiality destroys confidence. I could have applied to his reasoning what he opposed to mine, but if the laws of humanity prohibit striking one's fellows because it causes them harm, there is all the more reason not to wound their souls by expressing scorn for their opinions, and I contented myself with explaining my feelings to him without attacking his own.

Furthermore, a dearer interest was pressing me to change the subject of our conversation. I interrupted him as soon as possible to pose questions about the distance separating the city of Paris from that of *Cuzco* and about the possibility of making the journey. The *Cusipata* kindly satisfied my curiosity, and although he indicated to me the distance between these two cities in a most disheart-

---

[48]See *Histoire des Incas* [Garcilaso, *Royal Commentaries* 189–90; see translator's note on p. 14 and bracketed material in note 9].

ening fashion and made me regard as insurmountable the hardships involved in making such a journey, knowing that the thing was possible was enough to bolster my courage and give me the confidence to communicate my plan to the kind monk.

He appeared astonished by this plan and did his best to dissuade me from such an undertaking with words so sweet that he aroused in me pity for myself at the thought of the dangers to which I would be exposed; nevertheless, my resolve was not shaken in the least. I implored the *Cusipata* to inform me of the means by which to return to my homeland. He did not wish to go into any detail, saying only that Déterville, highly esteemed by virtue of his noble birth and personal merit, could do whatever he wished and that since he had an uncle who was all-powerful at the court of Spain, he could obtain for me news of our unfortunate regions more easily than anyone.

To convince me once and for all to await Déterville's return, which he assured me to be imminent, he added that in light of the obligations I had to this generous friend, I could not honorably dispose of my own person without his consent. I agreed to that and listened with pleasure to the speech he made me in praise of the rare qualities distinguishing Déterville from other persons of his rank. The burden of gratitude is quite light, dearest

Aza, when that burden has been received only from the hands of virtue.

This learned man also told me of how chance had brought the Spaniards to your unfortunate empire and that the thirst for gold was the sole cause of their cruelty. He then explained to me in what manner the law of war had caused me to fall into Déterville's hands through a battle from which he had emerged victorious after capturing several Spanish vessels, among which the one that had been carrying me.

In the end, dearest Aza, while he confirmed my misfortunes, at least he lifted me from the cruel darkness regarding so many dreadful events in which I had been living, and this has afforded me no small easing of my troubles. I am awaiting the rest from Déterville's return: he is humane, noble, virtuous; I must count on his generosity. If he returns me to you, what a good deed! What joy! What happiness!

XXII

Dearest Aza, I had been counting on making a friend of the learned *Cusipata*, but a second visit from him destroyed the high opinion I had formed of him during the first.

While he had initially appeared gentle and sincere to me, this time I found only harshness and duplicity in all that he told me.

With my mind peacefully settled on the interests of my tenderness, I wished to satisfy my curiosity concerning the wondrous men who make books. I began by inquiring about the rank they hold in the world, the reverence reserved for them, and finally the honors and tributes bestowed upon them for the great number of benefits they spread throughout society.

I do not know what about my questions the *Cusipata* found to be amusing, but he smiled at each one and made as his only reply to them such intemperate speeches that it was not difficult for me to see that he was deceiving me.

Indeed, if I am to believe him, these men, unquestionably superior to others by virtue of the nobility and usefulness of their work, are often left unrewarded and therefore obliged, in order to make their living, to sell their thoughts just as the common people sell the vilest products of the earth in order to survive. Can this really be?

Deceit, dearest Aza, scarcely displeases me less beneath the transparent mask of jocularity than it does under the thick veil of seduction. The monk's deceit offended me, and I did not deign to offer a reply to it.

Unable to satisfy that curiosity, I turned the conversation to the subject of my planned voyage, but rather than dissuading me from it with the same gentleness as the first time, he raised such strong and convincing objections that I found only my tenderness for you able to combat them and did not hesitate to confess this to him.

At first he took on a cheerful countenance and, appearing to doubt the truthfulness of my words, answered me only with mocking remarks that, however insipid they were, did not fail to insult me. I did my best to convince him of the truth, but as my heart's expressions proved the truth of its sentiments, his face and words grew severe. He dared tell me that my love for you was incompatible with virtue and that I had to give up one or the other, that is to say that loving you could only be a crime.

When I heard those senseless words, the most searing rage filled my soul, and I forgot the moderate tone I had prescribed for myself, insteading showering him with reproaches, telling him what I thought of the duplicity of his words, and maintaining over and over again that I will always love you. Then, without waiting to hear his apologies, I took leave of him and ran to my room, where, behind my closed door, I was sure he could not follow me.

Oh dearest Aza, how strange is the reason of this land! In general it acknowledges that the first and foremost virtues are doing good and being true to one's commitments, yet in particular it prohibits being true to those the purest sentiment has formed. It commands gratitude yet seems to stipulate faithlessness.

I would be praiseworthy were I to put you back on the throne of your forefathers, yet for maintaining for you a good far more precious than all the world's empires, I am criminal.

I would receive approval were I to give the treasures of Peru as recompense for your good deeds. Stripped of everything, dependent for everything, I possess only my tenderness. They wish me to rob you of it, for to be virtuous one must be faithless. Oh my dearest Aza! I would betray all notions of virtue were I to cease loving you for one moment. While being faithful to their laws, so shall I be to my love: I shall live only for you.

XXIII

I believe, dearest Aza, that only the joy of seeing you could be greater than that caused me by Déterville's return. But as if it were no longer permitted me to taste of it unadulterated, this one was soon followed by a sadness that still endures.

Yesterday morning Céline was in my room, when she was mysteriously summoned. She had not been gone long, when she had me told to come to the parlor. I raced to it: imagine my surprise at finding Déterville sitting there with her!

I made no effort to hide my pleasure at seeing him, for I owe him esteem and friendship. These sentiments are practically virtues, and I expressed them with as much truthfulness as I felt them.

I saw before me my liberator, sole support of my hopes. I was going to speak without restraint of you, of my tenderness, of my plans; my joy knew no bounds.

I did not yet speak French when Déterville departed. How many things did I not have to tell him? How many clarifications to seek, how much gratitude to express? I wanted to say everything at once, I spoke badly, and yet I was speaking a great deal.

As I spoke, I noticed that the sadness I had observed on Déterville's face as I came in had dissipated, giving way to joy. I congratulated myself on this change, which impelled me to go further in my efforts to effect it. Alas, should I have feared giving too much joy to a friend to whom I owe everything and on whom I am counting for all to come? Yet my sincerity threw him into a state of misunderstanding that is now costing me quite a number of tears.

Céline left the parlor at the same time I came in; perhaps her presence would have spared us such a cruel explanation.

Attentive to my words, Déterville seemed to be taking pleasure from hearing them without giving any thought to interrupting me. I was seized by a vague worry when I wanted to start asking him for information about my voyage and explaining to him its purpose. But while I, temporarily at a loss for the right expressions, was deciding what to say, he took advantage of a moment of silence to kneel before the grille he had gripped with both hands and say to me in an emotional voice: "To what sentiment, divine Zilia, am I to attribute the pleasure I see just as frankly expressed in your lovely eyes as in your speech? Am I the happiest of men at that very moment when my sister has just made me understand that I was the one most to be pitied?"

"I do not know what sorrow Céline could have caused you," I replied, "but I am quite certain that never will you be caused any by me."

"Yet she told me that I must hold no hope of ever being loved by you."

Interrupting him I cried out, "Never loved by me! Oh Déterville, how could your sister blacken my reputation with such a crime? Ingratitude fills me with horror, and I would hate myself were I to think myself capable of ceasing to love you."

While I was uttering those few words, he, to judge by the intentness of his gaze, seemed to be trying to read what was written in my soul, then said, "You love me, Zilia, and you are telling me so! I would give my life to hear that delightful confession, but alas, I cannot believe it even as I am hearing it! Zilia, dearest Zilia, is it really true that you love me? Are you not fooling yourself? Your tone, your eyes, and my heart all seduce me, but perhaps it is only to plunge me back down still more cruelly into the despair from which I am emerging."

"You shock me," I rejoined. "What is the origin of your lack of trust? Since I have known you, even if I have not been able to make myself understood in words, have not all my actions proven that I love you?"

"No," he riposted, "I can flatter myself no longer: you do not speak French well enough to dispel my well-founded fears. I know you are not trying to deceive me, but please explain to me what meaning you attach to those charming words 'I love you.' Let my fate be decided so that I might die at your feet of agony or of ecstasy."

Somewhat intimidated by the excitement with which he pronounced his last phrase, I told him, "Those words should, I believe, make you understand that you are dear to me, that your fate is of interest to me, that friendship and gratitude attach me to you. Those feelings are pleasing to my heart and should satisfy yours."

"Oh Zilia," he said in reply, "how your terms grow weaker and your tone colder! Might Céline have told me the truth? Is it not for Aza that you feel all that you say?"

"No," I told him, "the feeling I have for Aza is totally different from those I have for you. It is what you call love . . ."

Seeing him grow pale, let go of the grille, and turn grief-stricken eyes heavenward, I added, "What pain can that cause you? I have love for Aza because he has love for me and because we were to be married. None of that has any relation whatsoever to you."

"The very same you find there to be between you and him," Déterville burst out, "since I have a thousand times more love than he has ever felt from that bond."

"How could that be?" I answered back. "You are not at all of my nation, and far from having chosen me to be your wife, you know me only because of the sheer chance that brought us together; indeed, it is only starting today that we can even freely communicate our ideas. For what reason would you have the feelings for me of which you speak?"

"Need there be any reasons beside your charms and my character to attach me to you unto death?" he replied, then continued, "Born tender, idle, and an enemy of all artifice, I had only a vague and passing fancy for women in light of the difficulties I would have had to endure to penetrate their hearts and of my fear of not finding in them the honesty I desired. I lived without passion until the moment I saw you. I was struck by your beauty, but the impression made upon me might have been as light as that made by the beauty of many others had not the sweetness and naiveté of your character presented me with the object that my imagination had so often put before me. You know whether I showed respect for that object of my adoration, Zilia. What did it not cost me to resist the seductive opportunities offered me by the close quarters of a long sea voyage! How many times might your innocence have delivered you over to my transports of desire had I heeded them? But, far from giving you offense, I pushed discretion to the point of silence. I even demanded of my sister that she not speak to you of my love, for I wanted to owe nothing to anyone save you. Oh Zilia, if you are not the least bit moved by such tender regard, I shall flee you, but I sense already that my death will be the price of that sacrifice!"

"Your death!" I burst out, stabbed by the genuine pain with which I saw him burdened. "Alas, what a sacrifice! I know not whether that of my life would not be less dreadful for me."

"Well, Zilia," he told me, "if my life is dear to you, do you then order that I live?"

"What must be done?" I asked.

"Love me the way you loved Aza," he replied.

"I still love him the same way and will love him unto death," I rejoined, then added, "I do not know whether your laws permit you to love two persons in the same manner, but our customs and my heart forbid it. Be content with the sentiments I have promised you, for I cannot have any others. Truth is dear to me, and I am speaking it to you without embellishment."

"With what calm do you kill me!" he cried. "Oh Zilia, how I love you, for I adore even your cruel honesty. Well," he continued after keeping silent for a few moments, "my love will surpass your cruelty. Your happiness is dearer to me than my own. Make no effort to spare my feelings and speak to me with that sincerity that tears me apart. What is your hope for the love you maintain for Aza?"

"Alas," I told him, "all my hope rests with you alone!" I went on to explain to him how I had learned that communication with the Indies was not impossible and to tell him that I flattered myself to think that he would obtain for me the means of returning there, or at the very least that he would be good enough to have transported to you the knots that would inform you of my fate and to have brought back to me your replies so that, informed of your destiny, I might use it as a rule for my own.

With affected calm, Déterville told me, "I shall take the steps necessary to learn the fate of your beloved, so in that regard you will be satisfied. You would flatter yourself in vain, however, hoping to see that fortunate Aza again, for there are insurmountable obstacles separating you."

Those words, dearest Aza, were a mortal blow to my heart. Tears streamed down my face when I heard them, and for some time those tears prevented my replying to Déterville, who for his part maintained a mournful silence.

"Well," I finally said to him, "I shall never see him again, but I shall live for him all the same. If your friendship is generous enough to procure some form of correspondence for us, that satisfaction will be enough to make my life less intolerable, and I shall die contented, provided that you promise me to let him know that I died loving him."

He leapt to his feet and cried, "Oh, this is too much! Yes, if possible, I shall be the only unhappy one. You will come to know this heart you scorn, you will see of what efforts a love such as mine is capable, and I will force you at least to pity me."

After saying these words he walked out, leaving me in a state I still do not comprehend. I remained standing, eyes fixed on the door through which Déterville had just passed, floundering in a profusion of confused thoughts that I did not even attempt to untangle. I would have remained in that state for some time had not Céline entered the parlor.

She asked me in a brusque tone why Déterville had left so soon. I did not hide from her what had happened between us. First she lamented what she called her brother's misfortune. Then, turning her sorrow to anger, she rebuked me in the harshest possible terms. Troubled to the point of barely being able to think, I dared not offer one word in opposition, for what could I have said to her? I left the parlor and she made no move to follow me. I stayed shut up in my room for a day, not daring to show myself, not having any news of anyone, and in a disordered state of mind that would not even permit me to write you.

Céline's anger, her brother's despair, and his last words, to which I would like to ascribe a favorable meaning but dare not do so, each in turn delivered my soul over to the cruelest anxieties.

Finally I decided that the only way for me to ease my fears would be to depict them for you, to share them with you, to seek in your tenderness the counsel I need. This error sustained me while I was writing, but how briefly it endured! My letter is finished, and the characters composing it have been drawn solely for me.

You are unaware of what I am suffering, you do not even know if I exist, if I love you. Aza, dearest Aza, will you ever know?

XXIV

I could again call the time elapsed since last I wrote you an absence, dearest Aza.

A few days after my conversation with Déterville, I came down with an illness they call the *fever*. If, as I believe, it was caused by the painful passions stirred in me at that time, I have no doubt that it has been prolonged by the sad reflections now occupying my mind and by my regret at having lost Céline's friendship.

Although she has seemed to take an interest in my illness and has cared for me in all ways depending on her, she has done so in such a cold manner and with so little consideration for my soul that I cannot doubt the change in her feelings. The extreme friendship she has for her brother is setting her against me, and she blames me without cease for making him unhappy. Shame at seeming ungrateful intimidates me, Céline's affected kindness makes me uncomfortable, my discomfort inhibits her, and gentleness and pleasure are banished from our relations.

Despite so much vexation and unhappiness on the part of both brother and sister, I am not oblivious to the events changing their destinies.

Déterville's mother has died. That unnatural mother hardly stepped out of character—she gave all her assets to her elder son. It is hoped that the legal professionals will prevent this injustice from being carried out. Disinterested regarding himself, Déterville is taking infinite pains to rescue Céline from destitution. It seems that her misfortune has redoubled his friendship with her, for in addition to coming to see her every day, he writes her morning and night. His letters are full of such tender complaints against me and such anxious inquiries concerning my health that much as Céline pretends while reading them to wish only to inform me of the progress of their affairs, I easily discern her true motive.

I do not doubt that Déterville writes these letters only so that they may be read to me; nevertheless, I am convinced that he would desist were he to know of the reproaches that follow this reading, reproaches that make their impression on my heart. I am consumed with sadness.

Until now, amid all this turmoil, I enjoyed the slender satisfaction of living at peace with myself: no stain soiled the purity of my soul, no remorse troubled it. Now I cannot help but think with a kind of contempt for myself that I am making unhappy two people to whom I owe my life, that I am upsetting the tranquility they would be enjoying without me, that I am causing them all the harm it is in my power to cause, yet neither can nor want to cease being criminal. My tenderness for you triumphs over my remorse; oh Aza, how I love you!

XXV

How harmful caution is at times, dearest Aza. I long resisted the urgent requests Déterville had made me that I grant him a moment's audience. Alas, I was fleeing my happiness. Finally, less from a desire to be accommodating than from weariness at arguing with Céline, I allowed myself to be led to the parlor. I was stunned by the sight of the dreadful change that has left Déterville practically unrecognizable and was already repenting of my behavior as I trembled in anticipation of the reproaches I felt he had every right to make me. Could I have guessed that he was going to fill my soul with happiness?

"Forgive me, Zilia," he said, "for the violence I have done you. I would not have obliged you to see me were

I not bringing you as much joy as you cause me pain. Is seeing you for a moment too much to require in exchange for the cruel sacrifice I am making you?" Then, without giving me time to say a word in reply, he continued, "Here is a letter from that relative of whom you were told. By informing you of Aza's fate, it will prove more convincingly than all my vows how excessive my love is."

Having said this, he immediately read me the letter. Oh dearest Aza, could I have heard it without dying of joy? It informed me that your days have been preserved, that you are free, and that you are living in no danger at the court of Spain. What unexpected good fortune!

This wonderful letter was written by a man who knows you, sees you, speaks with you. Was your gaze perhaps even fixed on this precious sheet of paper for a moment? I could not take mine from it and was but barely able to restrain the shouts of joy ready to issue from me as tears of love inundated my face.

Had I followed my heart's impulse, I would have interrupted Déterville a hundred times to tell him all that my gratitude inspired in me, but in no way did I forget that my happiness would surely add to his pain; hence, I hid from him my transports, and he saw only my tears.

After he stopped reading, he said to me, "Well, Zilia, I have kept my word: you now know Aza's fate. If this is somehow not enough, what more must be done? Order without restraint, for there is nothing you have not the right to require of my love, provided it should contribute to your happiness."

Although I should have expected this excess of kindness, it surprised and touched me.

For a few moments I was confused as to how to respond, for I feared aggravating the pain of such a generous man. I tried to find words that would express my heart's truth without offending the sensibilities of his; unable to find them, I had to speak anyway.

"My happiness," I told him, "will never be unadulterated, since I cannot reconcile the duties of love with those of friendship. I would like to regain yours and Céline's, I would wish never to have to leave you, to admire your virtues without cease, and to repay each day of my life the tribute of gratitude that I owe to your goodness. I sense that in going away from two people so dear to me, I shall carry with me eternal regrets. But . . ."

"What!" cried Déterville. "You want to leave us! Oh Zilia, I was utterly unprepared for this grievous resolution. I lack the courage to withstand it. I had enough to see you here in the arms of my rival. The efforts of my reason and the thoughtfulness of my love had steeled me against that mortal blow; indeed, I would have brought it about myself. But I cannot part with you, I cannot give up seeing you. No," he continued angrily, "you shall not leave. Do not count on that. You are abusing my tenderness and mercilessly breaking a hopelessly love-lorn heart. Zilia, cruel Zilia, see my despair, for it is of your making. Alas, at what price do you repay the purest of loves!"

"It is you," I told him, terrified at his determination, "whom I should accuse. You brand my soul criminal by forcing it to be ungrateful. You oppress my heart through fruitless sensitivity. In the name of friendship, do not tarnish unprecedented generosity with a despair that will make my life bitter without bringing you happiness. Do not condemn in me the same sentiment you cannot overcome. Do not force me to complain of you. Let me cherish your name, bear it with me to the ends of the earth, and have it revered by peoples that worship virtue."

I do not know how I uttered those words, but Déterville, eyes fixed upon me, seemed not to be looking at me. Withdrawn into himself, he remained for some time in a deep meditation. For my part, I did not dare interrupt him. We were observing an equal silence when he resumed speaking, telling me with a kind of tranquility, "Yes, Zilia, I acknowledge, I sense the full measure of my unjustness. But does one calmly give up the sight of so many charms? You wish it so, you will be obeyed. Oh heavens above, what a sacrifice! My sad days will pass and come to their end without my seeing you! Unless death . . . But let us speak of this no more," he added, interrupting himself, "my weakness would betray me. Give me two days to steel myself. I will come back and see you, as it is necessary that we take certain measures together in preparation for your voyage. Farewell, Zilia. May the fortunate Aza sense the full measure of his happy fate!"

As he said this, he left the room.

I confess to you, dearest Aza, that much as Déterville is dear to me and much as I was penetrated by his sorrow, I was too impatient to enjoy my happiness in peace not to be quite delighted at his taking his leave.

How sweet it is, after so many troubles, to give oneself over to joy! I spent the rest of the day in the tenderest of raptures. I did not write you at all. A letter was too little for my heart—it would have reminded me of your absence. I was seeing you, I was speaking to you, dear Aza! What would my happiness have lacked had you attached to the precious letter I received some mark of your tenderness! Why did you not do so? Others have spoken to you about me, you have been informed of my fate, and nothing speaks to me of your love. But can I doubt your heart? My own answers for it. You love me, your joy is equal to mine, you burn with the same fires, the same impatience consumes you. May fear depart my soul, may unadulterated joy rule over it. And yet you have espoused the religion of that fierce people. What religion is it? Does it require that you renounce my tenderness, as the religion of France wished that I renounce yours? No, you would have rejected it.

Whatever the case may be, my heart is under your rule, subject to the lights of your reason, and I will adopt blindly all that should be capable of rendering us inseparable. What can I fear? I shall soon be reunited with my treasure, my being, my all; I shall think no more save by you, shall live no more save to love you.

XXVI

It is here, dearest Aza, that I will see you again. My happiness grows greater every day by virtue of its own reason for being. I have just left the interview that Déterville had granted me, and whatever pleasure I should have derived from overcoming the hardships of the journey, letting you know of my arrival, and running to meet you, I sacrifice without regret for the happiness of seeing you sooner.

Déterville presented me with such overwhelming evidence that you can be here in less time than it would take me to go to Spain that, much as he was generous enough to leave the choice to me, I did not hesitate to wait for you: time is too precious to waste it unnecessarily.

Perhaps I might have considered this advantage more carefully before making up my mind had I not obtained several clarifications concerning my voyage that caused me to come to my final decision for secret reasons I can confide only to you.

I remembered that during the long journey that brought me to Paris, Déterville gave out pieces of silver and sometimes of gold in all the places where we stopped. I wanted to know if he did this out of obligation or simple liberality. I learned that in France one makes travelers pay not only for their food but for their repose as well![49] Alas, I have not the least fraction of what would be required to content the avidity of this self-interested people and would have to receive it from the hands of Déterville. But could I resolve to contract voluntarily a kind of debt whose shame extends nearly to the point of disgrace? I cannot, dearest Aza. This reason alone would have determined me to remain here, and the pleasure of seeing you more promptly only served to strengthen my resolve.

Déterville wrote in front of me to the Spanish Minister, pressing him to send you forth with a generosity that filled me with gratitude and admiration.

What sweet moments I spent while Déterville was writing! What a pleasure it was to be occupied with arranging for your journey, to see the preparations for my happiness being made, to be in doubt of it no longer!

If at first it cost me a great deal to give up my plan of being the first to come, I must confess, dearest Aza, that

---

[49]Along their roads the Incas had established large houses where travelers were welcomed at no charge.

I now find a thousand sources of pleasure in the current arrangement that I had not noticed before.

Several aspects of my situation that seemed to me to have no value regarding moving my departure forward or back have now become interesting and agreeable to me. I was blindly following the inclination of my heart, forgetting that I was going to be seeking you amid those barbarous Spaniards, the very idea of whom grips me with horror. I take infinite satisfaction from the certainty of never seeing them again. Love's voice was extinguishing friendship's, and I now taste without remorse the sweetness of combining them. Furthermore, Déterville has assured me that it would be impossible for us ever to see the city of the Sun again. Next to our homeland, is there a more pleasant place to stay than France? You will like it, dearest Aza, for much as sincerity has been banished from the place, one finds so many amenities here that they make one forget about the dangers of society.

In light of what I have told you about gold, my warning you to bring some with you is unnecessary, and you have no use for other merits. The least portion of your treasures will suffice to win you admiration and to confound the pride of the haughty poor of this realm, but your virtues and sentiments will be prized only by Déterville and me. He has promised me to have my knots and letters delivered to you and has assured me that you could find interpreters to explain the latter to you. They are coming for the package, and so I must leave you. Farewell, dear hope of my life. I shall continue to write you, and if I am unable convey my letters to you, I shall keep them for you.

How could I bear the length of your voyage were I to deny myself the sole means I have of discussing my joy, my rapture, my happiness?

XXVII

Since knowing my letters to be on their way, dearest Aza, I have enjoyed a peace of mind I had ceased to know. I am constantly thinking of the pleasure you will take from receiving them, see your excitement, and share it. From all sides, my soul takes in only pleasant ideas, and to make my joy complete, peace has been reestablished in our little community.

The judges have restored to Céline the assets of which her mother had deprived her. She sees her suitor every day, and her marriage is being delayed only by the necessary preparations. Now that all her wishes are fulfilled, she no longer thinks of scolding me, and I am as obliged to her as I would be if I owed to her friendship the kindness she is again beginning to show me. We are always indebted to those who make us experience a sweet sentiment, no matter what their motive.

This morning she made me feel the full value of such behavior through an act of kindness that caused me to

113

pass from a disturbing state of anxiety to a pleasing sense of tranquility.

She was brought a prodigious quantity of textiles, clothing, and jewels of all kinds. She ran to my room and led me into hers where, after asking my opinion of the varying degrees of beauty of such a multitude of adornments, she herself heaped together those items that had most drawn my attention and was already eagerly ordering our *Chinas* to carry them to my room when I objected to what she was doing with all my might. At first my insistence served only to amuse her, but seeing that her determination was increasing with my refusals, I could not hide my resentment any longer.

"Why," I asked her, my eyes bathed in tears, "do you want to humiliate me more than I am already? I owe you my life and all that I have, which is more than enough to prevent my ever forgetting my misfortune. I know that, according to your laws, when that which is received is of no use to the recipient, the shame is erased, so wait until I have no more need of your generosity before exercising it. It is not without reluctance," I added in a more moderate tone, "that I conform to such unnatural sentiments. Our customs are more humane: the one who receives is honored as much as the one who gives. You have taught me to think otherwise. Was that only to dishonor me?"

This charming friend, more moved by my tears than annoyed by my reproaches, answered me in a friendly tone, "Dearest Zilia, my brother and I are far from wanting to wound your sense of propriety, and it would ill befit us to put on airs with you, for you shall soon know magnificence yourself. I wished only that you share with me the gifts of a generous brother, for it was the surest way to show him my gratitude. Custom, in my current condition, authorized my making you such an offer, but as it offends you, I shall speak of it no more."

"So you are promising me this?" I asked her.

"Yes," she replied with a smile, "but allow me to write a note to Déterville."

I let her do as she liked, and cheerfulness was reestablished between us. We went back to examining her finery more carefully until the moment when she was requested in the parlor. She wanted to bring me too, but for me, dearest Aza, are there any entertainments comparable to that of writing you? Far from seeking others, I dread those that Céline's marriage holds in store for me.

She would have me leave this convent to live in her home when she is married, but if I am believed in this matter . . .

Aza, dearest Aza, by what a pleasant surprise was my letter interrupted yesterday! Alas, I thought I had lost forever those precious monuments of our former splendor! I had ceased counting on them, ceased even thinking about them, and now I am surrounded by them; I see them, I touch them, yet I barely believe my eyes and hands.

As I was writing to you, I saw Céline come in followed by four men laboring under the weight of the large chests they were carrying. They put them down and left the room. I thought they might contain further gifts from Déterville and was already muttering to myself, when Céline told me as she was handing me the keys, "Open them, Zilia, open them and do not be shy—they are from Aza."

I believed this. At the sound of your name, is there anything that can put a stop to my eagerness? I hastened to open them, and my surprise reinforced my error, for I recognized all that lay before my eyes as ornaments from the temple of the Sun.

A confused feeling composed of sadness and joy, pleasure and regret filled my whole heart. I prostrated myself before those sacred remnants of our religion and our Altars, covered them with respectful kisses, bathed them with my tears. I could not tear myself away from them and had forgotten Céline's very presence when she drew me from my intoxication by handing me a letter, which she asked me to read.

Still immersed in my error, I believed it to be from you, and my excitement redoubled. Although I could only make it out with difficulty, however, I soon realized that it was from Déterville.

It will be easier for me, dearest Aza, to copy it for you than to explain to you its meaning.

These treasures are yours, fair Zilia, since I found them aboard the vessel that was carrying you. Some disagreement that arose among the crew prevented me from disposing of them freely until now. I wished to offer them to you myself, but the worries you expressed to my sister this morning no longer leave me any choice with regard to the timing, for I cannot dispel your fears too soon. All my life I shall prefer your satisfaction to mine.

I admit with embarrassment, dearest Aza, that at that moment I was less sensitive to Déterville's generosity than to the pleasure of giving proof of mine to him.

I promptly set aside a vase that chance more than greed had caused to fall into the hands of the Spaniards. It is this same vase—my heart recognized it—that your lips touched the day you wished to taste of the aca[50] made by my hand. Richer for this treasure than for all the others restored to me, I called over the persons who had carried them in and wished to have them take those other articles back to return them to Déterville. Céline, however, objected to my plan.

"How unfair you are, Zilia," she told me. "What! You wish to make my brother accept immense riches—you, who take offense at the offer of a mere trifle. Recall your own sense of fairness if you want to inspire it in others."

---

[50]Indian beverage.

Those words struck me, and I feared that there might be more pride and vengeance in my action than generosity. How close vices are to virtues! I admitted my mistake and begged Céline's pardon, but I was suffering too greatly from the constraint she wished to impose upon me not to seek some respect in which to ease it.

"Do not punish me as fully as I merit," I said to her timidly. "Do not shun a few examples of the work of our unfortunate regions. You have no need of it; hence, my entreaty should scarcely offend."

As I was speaking, I noticed that Céline was looking attentively at two finely crafted shrubs of gold filled with birds and insects. I hastened to offer them to her along with a little silver basket that I filled with the most perfect imitations of shells, fish, and flowers. She accepted this offering with a graciousness that delighted me.

I then chose several idols of nations vanquished[51] by your ancestors and a small statue[52] that represented a Virgin of the Sun. I added to these a tiger, a lion, and other courageous animals and asked her to send them to Déterville.

---

[51] The Incas had the idols of the peoples they subjugated placed in the temple of the Sun after having first made them accept the worship of the Sun. They had idols themselves, for the Inca *Huayna* consulted the idol of Rimace. *Histoire des Incas*, t. 1, p. 350 [Garcilaso, *Royal Commentaries* 575; see translator's note on p. 14 and bracketed material in note 9].

[52] The Incas decorated their houses with golden statues of all sizes, even some of gigantic proportions.

"Then write him," Céline said to me with a smile. "Without a letter from you, these gifts would be ill received."

I was too pleased to refuse anything and wrote all that my gratitude dictated. When Céline had left the room, I passed out small gifts to her *China* and mine and set aside something for my writing master as well. I finally tasted the delicious pleasure of giving.

I did not do so indiscriminately, dearest Aza. All that comes from you, all that has intimate ties with your memory in no way left my hands.

The golden chair[53] that was kept in the temple for the days the *Capa-Inca* your august father came to visit, set off to one side of my room in the manner of a throne, represents for me your grandeur and the majesty of your rank. The great figure of the Sun, which I myself saw torn from the temple by those perfidious Spaniards, hangs over it and arouses my veneration. I prostrate myself before it, my spirit adores it, and my heart is entirely yours. On either side of the throne I have placed the two palms you gave the Sun as an offering and as a token of the fidelity you had sworn to me, and they ceaselessly remind me of your tender oaths.

Flowers[54] and birds spread symmetrically throughout my room form in miniature the image of those magnificent

---

[53]The Incas sat only on chairs of pure gold.

[54]It has already been said that the gardens of the temple and of the houses of royalty were filled with all sorts of imitations made of gold and silver. The Peruvians imitated the very grass called *maïs*, of which they fashioned entire fields.

gardens where I so often communed with my idea of you. My contented eyes rest nowhere without recalling to my mind your love, my joy, my happiness—indeed, all that will ever make up the life of my life.

XXVIII

Unable to resist Céline's urgings, dearest Aza, I had to follow her, and for two days now we have been at her country house, where her marriage was celebrated upon our arrival.

With what violence and what regret was I not torn from my solitude! Scarcely had I the time to enjoy the sight of those precious ornaments that made this solitude so valuable to me when I was forced to abandon it. And for how long? I do not know.

The revelry and pleasures with which everyone here appears intoxicated make me regret still more the peaceful days I spent writing you, or at least thinking of you; however, I have never seen objects so new to me, so wondrous, and so prone to amuse me, and with the passable command of the country's language I now have, I could obtain clarifications as entertaining as they would be useful concerning all that is going on before my eyes, if only the noise and commotion left anyone calm enough to answer my questions. To this point, however, I have found no one kind enough to do so, and I am hardly less confused than I was upon arriving in France.

The men and women wear finery so splendid and so covered with useless decorations, and each and every person utters what they have to say so rapidly, that the attention I pay in an effort to listen to their words prevents my seeing them and that looking at them carefully prevents me from understanding them. I remain in a kind of daze that would no doubt add much to their merriment had they the leisure to notice, but they are so occupied with themselves that my astonishment escapes them. That astonishment is only too well founded, dearest Aza, for here I see marvels whose motive forces are impenetrable to my imagination.

I shall not speak to you of the beauty of this house that is nearly the size of a city, decorated like a temple, and full of a great number of pleasant trifles of which I see so little use made that I cannot help but think that the French have chosen superfluousness as the object of their worship; they devote to it their arts, which are so far above nature. These arts seem intended only to imitate nature, in fact they surpass it. Furthermore, the manner in which they use nature's products often seems superior to nature's own. They assemble in their gardens in a space that can nearly be taken in at a single glance the beauties that nature distributes with economy over the entire face of the earth, and the elements, subjugated by them, seem to present obstacles to their undertakings only to make their triumphs more brilliant.

The astonished earth is to be seen nourishing and rais-
ing in its bosom plants from the most distant climes
without any need or evident necessity save that of obey-
ing the arts and adorning the idol of the superfluous.
Water, so easy to divide, which seemingly has shape only
on account of the vessels containing it and whose natural
inclination is to follow all types of slopes, here finds itself
forced to leap suddenly into the air without guide or support by its own strength and for no other purpose than
pleasing the eyes.

Fire, dearest Aza, I have seen fire, that terrible element,
give up its destructive power to be directed, docile, by a
superior force into taking all forms assigned it, sometimes depicting a vast expanse of light against a sky dark-
ened by the sun's absence, and other times showing us
that divine star descended upon the earth with its fires,
performing its usual functions, endowed with its dazzling
light, and in a blaze that fools one's eyes and one's judgment. What art, dearest Aza! What men! What genius!
I have forgotten all that I heard and all that I saw of their
pettiness; in spite of myself I have lapsed back into my
earlier state of wonder.

XXIX

It is not without genuine regret, dearest Aza, that I pass
from wonder at the genius of the French to contempt for
the use they make of it. I took honest pleasure from judg-

ing this nation charming, but I cannot deny the evidence of its faults.

The commotion finally died down, I was able to pose questions, and they were answered—here that is all it takes to be told even more than one wants to know. With an honesty and frivolousness beyond all belief, the French reveal the secrets of the perversity of their manners. Upon making the slightest inquiry, one needs neither skill nor insight to discern that their unbridled taste for the superfluous has corrupted their reason, their hearts, and their spirit, that it has built illusory riches upon the ruins of the necessary, that it has substituted a veneer of politeness for good manners, and that it has replaced common sense and reason with the false sparkle of wit.

The great pretense among the French is to appear lavishly wealthy. Genius, the arts, and perhaps even the sciences all relate back to ostentation and contribute to the destruction of fortunes. And as if the fecundity of their genius were not enough to multiply the objects on which to apply it, I have it on their own authority that they contemptuously turn their backs on those solid, pleasant objects produced in abundance by France itself, instead extracting from all parts of the world and at great expense the fragile, useless furnishings that decorate their houses, the dazzling garments with which they are covered, and even the very food and drink of which their meals are composed.

Perhaps, dearest Aza, I would find nothing objectionable in the excess of this superfluousness if the French had treasures enough to satisfy this taste or if they only devoted to it that which remained to them after establishing their households based on honest comfort.

Our laws, the wisest ever given to man, permit certain decorations to each station in life. These decorations characterize birth and riches, and one could, strictly speaking, deem them superfluous. What seems criminal to me, therefore, is only the superfluousness born of the imagination's being left unchecked that cannot be maintained without failing to meet one's obligations to humanity and justice; in a word, the kind of which the French are idolaters and to which they sacrifice their tranquility and their honor.

There is only one class of citizens among them in a position to take its worship of this idol to the highest degree of splendor without failing in its duty to the necessary. Other highly placed persons wanted to imitate them but are only this religion's martyrs. What pain, what confusion, what travail, and all to support a level of spending beyond their means! There are few noblemen who do not apply more industry, finesse, and trickery to distinguishing themselves through frivolous opulence than their ancestors employed caution, valor, and skills useful to the State to render their own names illustrious. And do not think that I am exaggerating to impress you, dearest Aza, for every day I hear the young people indignantly contesting among themselves the glory of having invested the most subtlety and skill into the maneuvers they employ to obtain the superfluous objects with which they adorn themselves from the hands of those who work only so as not to lack the essentials.

What contempt would such men not inspire in me for the entire nation were I not also to know that the French sin more frequently for lack of a correct understanding of things than for lack of forthrightness. Their frivolousness almost invariably excludes reasoning, and among them nothing is serious, nothing is weighty. Perhaps none of them has ever reflected upon the dishonorable consequences of his behavior. One must appear rich. That is the fashion, the custom, one follows it. An obstacle appears, one surmounts it by unjust means and thinks oneself merely to have triumphed over a difficulty. But the illusion runs deeper.

In most houses, indigence and superfluousness are but one room apart. They share the day's occupations, but in most divergent ways. Mornings in the office, the voice of poverty is to be heard issuing from the mouth of a man paid to find the means of reconciling a lack of resources with false opulence. Sorrow and rancor preside over these discussions which normally conclude with the sacrifice of the necessary, slaughtered on the altar of the superfluous. During the rest of the day, after adopting different garb, the surroundings of another room, and practically the traits of another being, they are bedazzled by their own magnificence, act cheerful, and call themselves happy. They even go so far as to believe themselves rich.

I have noticed, however, that some of those who display their splendor with the most affectation do not always dare believe that they impress. Accordingly, they joke among themselves about their own poverty, happily insulting the memory of their ancestors, whose wise thrift contented itself with comfortable clothing and ornaments and furnishings appropriate to their income rather than their birth. It is said that their families and their domestics enjoyed a frugal, honest bounty. They provided doweries for their daughters and built on solid foundations the fortune of the heir to their name, setting aside as a reserve that which would be necessary to help out a friend or other unfortunate in need.

I will tell you this, dearest Aza: in spite of the absurd light in which they cast the manners of those bygone days, they so pleased me, and I found them to have so much in common with the frankness of our own customs that, allowing my mind to wander, I felt my heart leap each time as if, at the end of the telling, I would find myself among our dear citizens. But the moment I began to applaud such wise practices, the peals of laughter I drew upon myself dispelled my illusion, and I found myself surrounded by nothing but the senseless French of this time, who glory in their uncontrolled imaginations.

The same depravity that has transformed the solid assets of the French into so many useless trifles has not rendered the ties binding their society any less superficial. The most sensible among them, who groan at this depravity, have assured me that in the past, as among us, honor was in the soul and humanity in the heart. That may be, but at present, what they call politeness takes the place of sentiment for them. This politeness consists of countless words without meaning, marks of respect without esteem, and pains taken without affection.

In the great households, a domestic is responsible for fulfilling social obligations. Every day he makes a considerable journey to go tell one person of concern for his health, another that there is grieving over his suffering or rejoicing at his pleasure. When this domestic returns, no one listens to the replies he brings back. There is mutual agreement to hold to the form while placing no interest in it, and these attentions take the place of friendship.

Shows of respect are made in person and are pushed to the point of childishness. I would feel ashamed to tell you of them were it not necessary to know everything about so singular a nation. One would be failing to show respect to one's superiors and even to one's equals if, after completion of the meal one has just eaten with them in familiar circumstances, one were to satisfy the demands of an urgent thirst without having requested as many pardons as permissions. One is also not supposed to allow one's clothing to brush against that of an important personage, and it would be considered disrespectful to look at that person attentively, but it would be quite a bit worse if one failed to see this person at all. I would need more intelligence and memory than I possess to report to you all the frivolities given and taken as marks of consideration, which practically means esteem.

In regard to the abundance of words, you will one day hear for yourself, dearest Aza, how exaggeration that is disavowed immediately after being uttered is the inexhaustible source of conversation for the French. They rarely fail to add a superfluous compliment to one that was superfluous in the first place, making an effort to be convincing that is in no way successful. They protest the sincerity of the praises they are forever lavishing with extravagant flattery and reinforce their declarations of love and friendship with so many unnecessary terms that the sentiment itself goes utterly unrecognized.

Oh dearest Aza, how the little anxiousness I show to speak and the simplicity of my expressions must seem insipid to them! Nor do I believe my mind to inspire any more esteem in them. To gain any reputation in that regard, one must have given evidence of great shrewdness at seizing the various meanings of words and displacing their uses. One must draw the attention of those listening through the subtlety of often impenetrable thoughts or by burying their obscure nature under a plethora of frivolous expressions. I read in one of their best books: *The spirit of society consists in pleasantly saying nothing at all, in not allowing oneself to make the least sensible utterance unless one has it excused for the grace of its formulation, and, finally, in concealing reason whenever one is forced to produce it.**

What could I tell you that would prove to you more convincingly that common sense and reason, regarded as the mind's essential components, are held in contempt here, as is all that is useful? In the end, dearest Aza, rest assured that the superfluous reigns so supreme in France that those who have only honest fortunes are poor, only virtues plain, only common sense foolish.

XXX

The inclination of the French carries them so naturally to extremes, dearest Aza, that Déterville, though exempt from the better part of his nation's faults, shares in this one all the same. Not content to keep his promise no

---

*TRANSLATOR'S NOTE: The quotation is taken from Charles Pinot Duclos, *Considerations sur les mœurs* 'Observations on Manners' (1750), ed. F. C. Green (Cambridge: Cambridge UP, 1939) 103. Duclos was a close friend and literary adviser to Graffigny at the time she was writing the present work. The original quotation starts, "Le *bon ton*, dans ceux qui ont le plus d'esprit, consiste." '*Good taste*, in those who have the most wit, consists' and concludes, "avec autant de soin que la pudeur en exigeoit autrefois, quand il s'agissoit d'exprimer quelque idée libre" 'with as much care as modesty required in days of old when it was a question of expressing some libertine notion.'

longer to speak to me of his feelings, he makes a great point of avoiding finding himself next to me. While we are forced to see each other constantly, I have not yet found an occasion to talk to him.

Although those present are always most numerous and most cheery, sadness rules his countenance. It is easy to divine that it is not without a struggle that he submits to the law he has imposed upon himself. I ought perhaps to take this into account, but I have so many questions to ask him concerning my heart's interests that I cannot forgive him his affectation of fleeing me.

I would like to ask him about the letter he sent to Spain and find out if it could have arrived by now. I would like to have an accurate idea of the time of your departure and of how long your journey will take so as to be able to fix the moment of my happiness. A well-founded hope is a genuine asset, dearest Aza, but it is much more valuable when one sees the point at which it will be realized.

None of the pleasures that occupy the others here affect me, being too tumultuous for my soul, and I no longer enjoy conversation with Céline. She is entirely occupied with her new husband, and it is only with difficulty that I can find a few moments in which to pay her the respects friendship requires. The rest of those present are only agreeable to me insofar as I can obtain enlightenment from them concerning the various objects of my curiosity, and I do not always find occasion to do so.

Thus, often alone while surrounded by people, I have no amusements save my thoughts: they are all yours, dear friend of my heart. Forever will you be the only confidant of my soul, of my pleasures, and of my troubles.

XXXI

I was very wrong, dearest Aza, to desire so ardently an interview with Déterville. Alas, he talked to me only too much, and although I disavow the turmoil he stirred in my soul, it has still not disappeared in the least.

Some kind of impatience joined itself yesterday to the boredom I often feel. The throng of other people and the noise vexed me more than usual. Everything I saw, down to the tender satisfaction of Céline and her husband, inspired in me an indignation verging on contempt. Ashamed at finding such unfair sentiments in my heart, I went to hide the consternation they were causing me in the farthest corner of the garden.

Scarcely had I sat down at the foot of a tree when unbidden tears poured from my eyes. Head buried in my hands, I was shrouded in such a deep reverie that Déterville was kneeling beside me before I noticed him.

"Do not take offense, Zilia," he told me, "it was chance that brought me to your feet. I was not looking for you. Bothered by the commotion, I left to savor my pain in peace. I noticed you and struggled with myself to move away, but I am too unhappy to be so without respite. Out of pity for myself I drew near. When I saw your tears flowing, I ceased to be master of my heart, but if you order me to leave you, I will obey. Are you capable of that, Zilia? Am I hateful to you?"

"No," I replied, "on the contrary. Sit down, I am quite pleased to have an opportunity to explain myself. Ever since your last acts of kindness . . ."

Interrupting me, he said, "We hardly need speak of that."

"Wait," I rejoined, interrupting him in turn; "to be thoroughly generous, one must be open to gratitude, and I have not spoken to you at all since you returned to me those precious ornaments belonging to the temple from which I was taken. Perhaps in writing you, I poorly expressed the feelings that such extreme goodness inspired in me. I wish . . ."

"Alas," he said, interrupting again, "how little does gratitude flatter an unhappy heart! Companion to indifference, it is joined only too often by hatred."

"What do you dare think?" I cried. "Oh Déterville, how severely would I chastise you were you not so worthy of pity! Far from hating you, from the first moment I saw you, I felt less revulsion at being subject to you than to the Spaniards. From then on your sweetness and your kindness made me wish to gain your friendship, and the more I came to know your character, the more that desire grew. I became certain that you merited all of my friendship and, without speaking of the great extent to which I am in your debt, since my gratitude offends you, how could I have helped having those sentiments that are your due?

"I found only your virtues worthy of the simplicity of ours. A son of the Sun could take pride in having your sentiments. Your reason is practically that of nature. How many grounds there are for cherishing you! I find pleasing everything about you down to the nobility of your features, for friendship has eyes as well as love. Before, after a moment of your absence, I never saw you return without feeling a kind of serenity spread throughout my heart. Why have you changed those innocent pleasures into pain and constraint?

"Your reason now appears only with effort, and I am forever fearing its lapses. The feelings of which you tell me hinder the expression of my own and deprive me of the pleasure of painting for you without indirection the charms I would savor through your friendship were you not to trouble its sweetness. You take from me everything down to the exquisite delight of looking upon my benefactor, for your eyes embarrass mine, and I no longer observe in them that agreeable tranquility that at times would penetrate all the way to my soul. Now I find in them nothing more than a mournful sorrow that blames me without cease for being its cause. Oh Déterville, how unjust you are if you believe you suffer alone!"

"My dear Zilia," he cried, kissing my hand with ardor, "how your kindnesses and your honesty redouble my regrets! What a treasure is the possession of a heart such as yours! But with what despair do you make me feel its loss!"

"Mighty Zilia," he continued, "what a power is yours! Was it not truly enough to make me pass from profound indifference to excessive love, from indolence to frenzy? Must sentiments you caused to be born now be vanquished? Will I be able to do so?"

"Yes," I told him, "that effort is worthy of you and of your heart. That just deed raises you above mortal men."

"But will I be able to survive it?" he asked in evident pain. "At least do not expect that I shall serve as victim of your lover's triumph. I will go far from you to adore the idea of you—it will serve as my heart's bitter sustenance. I will love you, and I will see you no more! Oh, at least do not forget . . ."

Sobs choked his voice, and he hastened to hide the tears that were covering his face. I was shedding tears as well, and, touched as much by his generosity as by his pain, I took one of his hands and clasped it in both of mine.

"No," I told him, "you will surely not leave. Let me be, my friend, content yourself with those feelings I will have for you all my life. I love you nearly as much as I love Aza, but I can never love you as I love him."

"Cruel Zilia," he cried out excitedly, "will you always accompany your kindnesses with the most telling blows? Will a lethal poison perpetually destroy the charm you spread over your words? How foolish I am to give myself over to their sweetness! Into what shameful abasement do I plunge!"

Then he added in a firm tone, "There, it is done, I am becoming myself again. Farewell. You will soon see Aza. May he not make you feel the torments that are devouring me. May he be as you desire him and worthy of your heart."

What alarm, dearest Aza, did the way in which he pronounced those last words not cast into my soul! I could not resist the host of suspicions that flocked to my mind. I did not doubt that Déterville, better informed than he wished to appear, might well have hidden from me letters that he could have received from Spain, or even that—dare I say it—you might have been unfaithful.

I implored him to tell me the truth, but all I could draw from him were vague conjectures just as apt to confirm my fears as to dispel them. Moreover, the reflections he made concerning men's inconstancy, the dangers of absence, and the lightheartedness with which you changed religion cast some uneasiness into my soul.

For the first time my tenderness became a painful sentiment for me, for the first time I feared losing your heart. Aza, if it was true! If you did not love me anymore . . . oh, may such a suspicion never sully the purity of my heart! No, I alone would be guilty if I lingered for a moment on this thought unworthy of my candor, of your virtue, of your fidelity. No, it is despair that suggested such dreadful ideas to Déterville. Should not his inner turmoil and distraction reassure me? Should not the self-interest that made him speak be suspect to me? So it was, dearest Aza: my consternation turned entirely against him; I treated him harshly; he left me in despair. Aza, I love you so tenderly! No, you could never forget me!

XXXII

How long your journey is, dearest Aza! How ardently I desire your arrival! Its end seems more vague than I had previously imagined, and I am being careful not to ask Déterville any questions about it. I cannot forgive him the poor opinion he has of your heart, and the one I am forming of his has greatly diminished the pity I had for his troubles and my regret at being in some sense separated from him.

We have been in Paris for two weeks. I am living with Céline in her husband's house, which is far enough away from her brother's that I am in no way obliged to see him at any hour of the day. He often comes here to take his meals, but Céline and I lead such a hectic life that he has no opportunity to speak with me privately.

Since returning, we spend a portion of the day on the dreary task of attiring ourselves and the rest on what is called doing one's duty.

These two occupations would seem to me as fruitless as they are tiresome were the latter not to provide me with means of learning about the manners of this country in still greater detail. When I first arrived in France, having no knowledge of the language, I judged only by appearances. When I first started speaking French, I was in that convent where, as you know, I received little help with my learning. In the country, I saw only a particular kind of people. At present, moving in what is called high society, I see the entire nation and can examine it without impediment.

The duties we perform consist of entering in one day the greatest number of houses possible, there to give and receive tributes of mutual praise for beauty of face and figure, for excellence of taste and choice of adornments, and never for qualities of soul.

I did not go long without realizing the reason for taking such pains to obtain this frivolous homage: it absolutely must be received in person, and even then it is highly ephemeral. The moment one disappears, it takes another form. The charms found in the woman leaving are no longer used for anything save contemptuous comparison to establish the perfections of the one who is arriving.

Censure is the dominant taste of the French, just as inconsistency is their national trait. Their books are general critiques of manners, and their conversations particular ones of each individual, provided nonetheless that those individuals are absent. Accordingly, one freely speaks all the ill one thinks of others, and sometimes ill one does not think. The best people follow this custom. One distinguishes them only by a certain formulaic insistence on their frankness and love of the truth, in the course of which they reveal without scruple the faults, the absurdities, and even the vices of their friends.

If the sincerity the French show toward one another is without exception, so too their mutual sharing of confidences is without limit. One needs neither eloquence to be heard nor probity to be believed. All is said and taken in with the same frivolousness.

Do not believe for all that, dearest Aza, that the French are born mean-spirited, for I would be less fair than they were I to leave you with such a misimpression.

Naturally sensitive and moved by virtue, they are, without exception that I have seen, tender listeners to the account I am frequently compelled to give of the forthrightness of our hearts, the candor of our sentiments, and the simplicity of our manners. Were they to live among us, they would become virtuous, for example and custom are the tyrants ruling their behavior.

This one thinks well of another not present but speaks ill of that person so as not to be scorned by those listening; that one would be good, humane, and without vainglory were he not to fear appearing ridiculous; and a third, ridiculous on account of his station, would be a model of perfection if he dared display his merit.

Finally, dearest Aza, in the majority of them, vice is as artificial as virtue, and the frivolity of their characters permits them to be only imperfectly what they are. Rather like certain of their childhood toys that are ill-defined imitations of thinking beings, they have weights on their eyes, are light to the touch, brightly colored on the surface, unformed on the inside, and seemingly have a price but are of no real value. Thus they are scarcely esteemed by other nations save as are pretty trifles in society. Common sense smiles at their genteel civilities and coldly puts them back in their place.

Fortunate is the nation having only nature for its guide, truth for its principle, and virtue as its driving force.

instead of nation person-Zilia novel-

XXXIII

It is not surprising, dearest Aza, that inconsequent behavior should be a result of the frivolous character of the French, but I never cease to be amazed that with as much and more enlightenment than any other nation, they seem not to perceive the shocking contradictions that foreigners notice in them at first glance.

Among the great number of these contradictions that strike me every day, I see none more dishonorable for their spirit than their manner of thinking about women. They respect them, dearest Aza, and at the same time hold them in equally great contempt.

The first law of their code of manners, or their virtue if you like (for to this point I have hardly discovered in them any others), concerns women. A man of the highest rank owes consideration to a woman of the basest possible standing. He would bring shame and what is called ridicule upon himself were he to make her any personal insult. Yet the least significant, least admired man can mislead and betray a woman of quality, blacken her reputation with slander, and have no fear of receiving blame or punishment.

If I were not certain that you will soon be able to judge for yourself, would I dare depict for you stark contrasts of which the simplicity of our minds can scarcely conceive? Receptive to nature's ideas, our genius does not go beyond them. We have found that strength and courage in one sex indicated that it should be the support and defender of the other, and our laws conform to that notion.[55] Here, far from sympathizing with the weakness of women, those from among the common people, overwhelmed by labor, are afforded relief neither by the law

---

[55]Their laws exempted women from all heavy labor.

nor by their husbands. Those of higher status are play-things of the seduction and wickedness of men and receive as compensation for being betrayed by them only the surface appearance of a purely imaginary respect, invariably followed by the most mordant satire.

Upon my entry into society, I already noticed that this nation's usual censure fell primarily on women and that among themselves men only showed contempt for one another in moderation. I was seeking the reason for this among their good qualities, when an unexpected incident caused me to discover it among their faults.

In all the households we have entered for the last two days, there has been talk of the death of a young man killed by one of his friends, and this barbaric deed has met with approval solely because the dead man had spoken to the survivor's detriment. This new eccentricity seemed of a serious enough nature to me to warrant fuller understanding. When I inquired further, dearest Aza, I learned that a man is obliged to risk his life to rob another of his if he learns that this other man has spoken any words against him or to banish himself from society should he refuse to take such cruel vengeance. It took no more than knowing this fact to open my eyes to what I was seeking. It is clear that men, naturally cowardly, without shame and without remorse, fear only bodily punishment and that if women were authorized to pun-ish the outrageous acts committed against them in the same manner that men are required to avenge the least serious insult, such men as are now seen and received in society would be no more, or they would be found only in some barren exile where they would hide their shame and bad faith. Brazen effrontery predominates among the young men, especially when they risk nothing. No further light need be shed on the reason for their behavior toward women, but I do not yet see the basis for the inner contempt for women that I notice in the minds of nearly everyone. I shall make an effort to discover it, for my own self-interest impels me to do so. Oh my dearest Aza! How great would be my pain if, when you arrive, I were to be spoken of as I hear others spoken of.

XXXIV

It has taken me a long time, dearest Aza, to deepen my understanding of the reason for the contempt in which almost everyone here holds women. I believe I have finally uncovered it in the slight relation between what women are and what it is imagined they ought to be. Here it is wished, as elsewhere, that women possess merit and virtue. But nature would have had to make them thus, for the upbringing they are given is in such opposition to the goal proposed that it appears to me to be the great masterpiece of French inconsequence.

In Peru, dearest Aza, we know that to prepare humans for the practice of virtue, one must inspire in them from childhood valor and a certain steadfastness of spirit that form in them a decisive character. This is unknown in France. From the earliest age, children appear destined only for the amusement of their parents and those who look after them. The French seem to wish to take shameful advantage of children's inability to discover the truth. They mislead their children regarding that which they do not see. They give them false notions regarding what they perceive with their senses and laugh mercilessly at their mistakes. They contribute to their children's natural oversensitivity and weakness through childish compassion for the little accidents that befall them, forgetting that these children must one day grow to be men.

I do not know what additional upbringing a father gives his son, having not informed myself in that regard. But I do know that, from the moment girls begin to be able to receive instruction, they are enclosed in a convent to be taught how to live in the world. The responsibility for the enlightenment of their minds is entrusted to persons in whom intelligence might be held a crime and who are incapable of educating their charges in matters of the heart, of which they know nothing.

Religious principles, so apt to serve as the germ of all virtues, are learned but superficially and by rote. Duties owed the divinity are not motivated in any more logical way and consist solely of little ceremonies imposed from outside that are required with such severity and practiced so lackadaisically that they are the first yoke to be shed upon entering the world. And should one preserve a few of its customs, to judge by the manner in which they are performed, one would readily believe them a mere politeness offered to the divinity out of habit.

Furthermore, nothing comes along to replace those first foundations of a misguided upbringing. In France, the self-respect with which we go to such pains to fill the hearts of our young Virgins is practically unknown. Here this generous sentiment, which makes of us the harshest judges of our own thoughts and deeds and becomes a reliable principle when it is truly felt, is unavailable to women. Going by the little attention devoted to women's souls, one would be tempted to believe that the French are prey to the error of certain barbarous peoples who deny them one.

Regulating body movement, controlling facial expressions, and composing exterior appearance are the essential points of their education. It is based on the more or less painfully constricted bearing of their daughters that parents glory in having raised them well. These parents counsel their daughters to be full of consternation over a violation of social grace. They do not tell them that an honest countenance is mere hypocrisy if it does not result from honesty of spirit. Forever being stirred in them is a contemptible form of self-love that affects only external charms. They are not made acquainted with that kind of self-love that forms merit and is only satisfied by esteem. The only idea of honor given them is limited to that of not having lovers. Meanwhile, they are constantly being offered the certainty of being found attractive as recompense for the painful constraint imposed upon them. And the most precious time for forming the mind is spent on acquiring imperfect talents that are seldom used in youth and become sources of ridicule at a more advanced age.

But that is not all, dearest Aza, for the inconsequent behavior of the French knows no limits. Starting from such principles, they expect their women to practice virtues with which they do not acquaint them; indeed, they do not even give them an accurate idea of the terms that designate them. Every day I gain clearer information about this situation than I need from the conversations I have with young persons whose ignorance causes me no less amazement than everything else I have seen until now.

If I speak to them about feelings, they deny having any because they are acquainted only with that of love. They understand by the word goodness only the natural compassion one feels at the sight of suffering, and even in that regard, I have noticed that they are more affected by animals than humans, but the tender, carefully considered goodness that causes one to do as one should with nobility and discernment and that leads to tolerance and humane forbearance is utterly unknown to them. They believe themselves to have fulfilled the entire range of discretion's obligations by revealing only to a few friends the frivolous secrets they have happened upon or had confided in them, but they have no notion of that circumspect, delicate discretion that is necessary not to be any burden, not to hurt others, and to help maintain social harmony.

If I attempt to explain to them what I mean by moderation, without which virtues themselves are practically vices, if I speak to them of decency of manners, of treating one's inferiors with consideration—something little done in France—and of steadfastly shunning those of base quality, I notice from their embarrassment that they suspect me of speaking Peruvian and that only politeness compels them to pretend to understand me.

They are no better informed about the world, men, and society. They do not even know the proper usage of their native language. Rarely do they speak it correctly, and I have noticed not without great surprise that I am now more expert than they in that regard.

It is in this kind of ignorance that girls are married barely out of childhood. The small interest their parents take in their conduct from then on would seem to indicate that they no longer belong to their parents. Most husbands take no more care of them. There would still be time to make good the flaws in their initial education, but no one takes the trouble.

Free in her apartment, a young woman can receive without restriction whomever she likes there. Her occupations are usually childish, always pointless, and perhaps even beneath idleness. Her mind is engaged by others in conversation at the very least about malicious or insipid frivolities more apt to make her contemptible than stupidity itself. Lacking confidence in her, her husband makes no effort to educate her in the care of his affairs, his family, or his household. She participates in this entire little universe only through appearances. She is a decorative figure to amuse the curious; accordingly, should even the slightest bit of imperiousness be added to her taste for dissipation, she will stumble into all kinds of trouble, quickly falling from independence to licentiousness, and will soon elicit men's scorn and indignation despite their inclination toward and interest in tolerating the vices of youth in tribute to its attractions.

Dearest Aza, though I am telling you the truth with all the sincerity of my heart, do not be misled into believing that there are no women of merit here, for there are some who are fortunate enough to be born able to give themselves what their upbringing has denied them. Their devotion to duty, decency of manner, and honest charms of mind draw everyone's esteem upon them. But their number is so limited in comparison to the multitude that they are known and revered by their own names. Nor should you believe that the disorder in the conduct of the others comes from a bad natural disposition. In general it seems to me that women here are born much more frequently than in our homeland with all the attributes necessary to equal men in merit and virtue. Seemingly conceding this equality in the bottom of their hearts but unable to tolerate it on account of their pride, men here do all they can to make women contemptible by either showing a lack of respect for their own wives or seducing those of others.

When you learn that here power is vested entirely in men, you will have no doubt, dearest Aza, that they are the ones responsible for all of society's disorders. Those who, out of lax indifference, leave their wives to continue to pursue the taste that proves to be their downfall, while not the most guilty, are not the least worthy of being scorned. Not enough attention is paid, however, to those who, through their example of base, indecent conduct, carry their wives along with them into the worst excesses, be it out of spite or vengeance.

And indeed, dearest Aza, how could these women not be revolted by the injustice of laws that tolerate men's impunity, which is pushed to the same extreme as their authority? A husband can, without fearing any punishment, treat his wife in the most repellent manner, dissipate on extravagances as criminal as they are excessive not only his assets and those of his children but those of his victim as well while making her groan in near indigence through his miserliness in matters of honest expenses—a trait very frequently found allied here with prodigality. He is authorized to punish harshly the appearance of a slight infidelity while abandoning himself shamelessly to all those that libertinage suggests to him. In the end, dearest Aza, it seems that in France the bonds of marriage are reciprocal only at the moment the wedding is celebrated and that thereafter only wives must be subject to them.

I think and feel that it would be honoring these women a great deal to believe them capable of keeping alive love for their husbands despite the indifference and distasteful behavior with which most of them are burdened. But who can withstand contempt!

The first feeling that nature put in us is the pleasure of being, and we feel that pleasure more keenly in proportion to the seriousness with which we sense ourselves to be taken.

The mechanical happiness of the earliest years comes from being loved by one's parents and welcomed by strangers. Happiness during the rest of one's life comes from sensing the importance of our being in proportion to its becoming necessary to the happiness of another. Dearest Aza, it is you and the great extent of your love, the frankness of our hearts, and the sincerity of our feelings that have revealed to me the secrets of nature and of love. Friendship, that wise and kindly bond, should perhaps fulfill all our wishes, but it shares its affection without crime or scruple among several objects. Love, which gives and requires an exclusive preference, presents us with such an elevated, satisfying concept of our being that it alone is able to content the avid ambition for primacy that is born with us, an ambition that manifests itself in all ages, in all eras, in all states, and our natural taste for ownership then completes the process of inclining us toward love.

If possessing a piece of furniture, a jewel, or a parcel of land is one of the most pleasurable feelings we experience, what must that one be like ensuring us of the possession of a heart, a soul, a free, independent being giving itself voluntarily in exchange for the pleasure of possessing in us those same advantages!

If it is therefore true, dearest Aza, that our hearts' dominant desire is to be honored in general and cherished by someone in particular, can you conceive of what inconsequential thinking could make the French able to expect that a young woman burdened by her husband's offensive indifference would not seek to escape this kind of annihilation presented to her in all manner of forms? Can you imagine how one could propose to her that she count on nothing in an age when claims always outstrip merit? Could you understand on what basis one would require of her the practice of virtues with which men dispense while refusing to offer her the enlightenment and principles necessary to practice them? But what is even harder to conceive is the way parents and husbands complain to one another of the contempt for their wives and daughters while at the same time perpetuating its cause from generation to generation through ignorance, lack of ability, and poor education.

Oh my dear Aza! May the glittering vices of a nation so seductive in other ways not cause us to lose in any way our taste for the natural simplicity of our manners! May you never forget your obligation to be my example, my guide, and my support along the path of virtue, and may I never forget mine to maintain your esteem and your love by imitating my model.

XXXV

Our visits and exertions, dearest Aza, could not have come to a more pleasing end. What a delightful day I spent yesterday! How pleasant are my new obligations to Déterville and his sister! But how dear will they be to me when I can share them with you!

After two days of rest, Céline, her brother, her husband, and I left Paris yesterday morning. She said that we were going to visit her very best friend. The journey was not long, and we arrived quite early in the day at a country house whose location and surroundings appeared marvelous to me. What surprised me on going inside, however, was finding all its doors open and no one there.

Too beautiful to be abandoned and too small to conceal those who should have lived in it, the house seemed an enchantment to me. This thought amused me, and I asked Céline if we were in the home of one of those fairies of whom she had had me read tales in which the mistress of the house is invisible, as are her domestics.

"You will see her," she told me, "but since important business has called her away for the entire day, she asked me to request that you perform the duties of host in her home while she is out," then added, "but first of all, you must, as I am sure you will, sign your consent to this proposal."

"Oh, with pleasure!" I told her, playing along with the joke.

No sooner had I uttered these words than I saw a man dressed in black enter the house. He was holding a writing case and paper already covered with writing which he handed to me and to which I added my name in the place where they wanted me to.

At that very instant appeared another man of pleasant enough countenance who invited us, as is the custom, to accompany him into the place where one eats. There we found a table laid as neatly as it was magnificently. We had scarcely sat down when most charming music could be heard in the adjoining room. Nothing was lacking of all that can make a meal pleasant. Even Déterville seemed to have forgotten his sorrow to incite us to be merry. He spoke to me in a thousand ways of his feelings for me, but always in a flattering tone without complaint or blame.

The day was calm, and by mutual agreement we decided to take a walk when we rose from the table. We found the gardens much more extensive than the house would lead one to expect. Their art and symmetry drew admiration only so as to render more evocative the charms of unadorned nature.

We brought our walk to an end in the wood that delimits this beautiful garden. All four of us were seated on a delightful lawn when we saw approaching from one side a troupe of peasants dressed neatly in their usual manner preceded by a few musical instruments and from the other a troupe of young girls dressed in white, heads adorned with wild flowers, who were singing in rustic but melodious fashion songs in which I was surprised to hear my name frequently repeated.

The two troupes joined us, and my astonishment grew much greater when I saw the most conspicuous of the men leave his group, kneel on the ground, and present me several keys in a large bowl with a compliment that my confusion kept me from hearing properly. I understood only that as leader of the area's villagers, he was coming to pay his respects to me in my capacity as their sovereign and to present me with the keys to the house of which I was also the mistress.

As soon as he had finished giving this official speech, he stood up to make room for the prettiest of the young girls. She stepped forward and offered me a spray of flowers decorated with ribbons that she also accompanied with a little speech in my honor that she delivered most graciously.

I was too taken aback, dearest Aza, to reply to praises I so little merited. Furthermore, all that was happening had a tone so close to that of reality that at many a moment I could not help believing what I nonetheless found unbelievable. That thought produced a whole host of others, and my mind was so occupied that it was impossible for me to utter a single word. If my consternation was amusing to the rest of those present, it was so embarrassing for me that Déterville was moved by it. He made a sign to his sister, who first gave a few gold pieces to the peasants and young girls, telling them that these were the first of what would be my many kind actions on their behalf, then rose and proposed to me that we take a stroll in the wood. I gladly followed her, fully intending to reproach her for the embarrassing situation in which she had put me, but I did not have the time. We had barely taken a few steps when she stopped and, beaming at me, said, "Admit it, Zilia, you are quite angry with us, and you will be even angrier if I tell you it is true that this estate and this house belong to you."

"To me," I cried. "Oh Céline, is this what you promised me? You are pushing this insult or joke too far."

"Wait," she said to me in a more serious tone. "If my brother had disposed of a portion of your treasures to purchase it while reserving for you not the annoying formalities to which he has attended but only the surprise, would you hate us so very much? Could you not forgive us for having procured a dwelling for you, which in any event you would seem to like, and for having ensured you an independent life? This morning you signed an authentic contract putting you in possession of both. Scold us now as much as you like," she added with a laugh, "if any of that is not agreeable to you."

"Oh, my dear, dear friend!," I cried as I threw myself into her arms, "I feel such generous attentions too keenly to tell you how grateful I am."

I was able to utter only those few words, for I had immediately sensed the significance of such a favor. I was touched, moved, and elated thinking about the pleasure I would have in devoting this charming dwelling to you, and the multitude of my feelings stifled their expression. I gave Céline caresses that she reciprocated with like tenderness. After allowing me adequate time to recover myself, we went and found her brother and her husband.

As I drew near Déterville, I was gripped by a new discomfort that inhibited my expressions anew. I offered him my hand. He kissed it without uttering a word, then turned away to hide tears he could not hold back; I took these for signs of his satisfaction at seeing me so happy and was moved to the point of shedding a few myself. Céline's husband, less interested than we in what was happening, soon put a light tone back into the conversation. He complimented me on my new rank and urged us to make our way back to the house, saying it was to examine its faults and show Déterville that his taste was not as impeccable as he flattered himself to think.

I will confess to you, dearest Aza, that all that lay before me as I passed appeared to me to take on a new form: the flowers seemed more beautiful, the trees greener, the symmetry of the gardens more highly ordered. I found the house cheerier, the furnishings richer. The least trifles had become interesting to me.

I glanced over all the rooms intoxicated with a joy that did not permit me to examine anything carefully. The only place I stopped was a rather large chamber surrounded by a delicately worked golden grille that held countless books of all colors, shapes, and sizes, which were in admirable condition. I was so enchanted that I thought I would be unable to leave them without having read them all. Céline tore me away by reminding me of a golden key that Déterville had handed me. I used it to open hastily a door that was pointed out to me, then stood frozen at the sight of the wonders it held.

Behind the door lay a study glittering with mirrors and paintings. The paneling was decorated with extremely well drawn figures against a green background. These figures imitated a portion of the games and ceremonies of the city of the Sun more or less as I had depicted them for Déterville.

In a thousand places on this paneling were representations of our Virgins wearing the same attire I had when I arrived in France. It was even said that they resembled me.

Supported by golden pyramids, the decorations from the temple that I had left in the convent adorned every corner of this magnificent study. The brilliance of the figure of the Sun, hanging from the middle of a ceiling painted the most beautiful colors of the heavens, put the finishing touches on the embellishment of this charming place of solitude, and comfortable furnishings that matched the paintings made it thoroughly delightful.

Taking advantage of the silence in which my surprise, joy, and admiration held me, Déterville drew near and told me, "You will surely notice, fair Zilia, that the chair of gold is nowhere to be found in this new temple of the Sun. A magical power has transformed it into a house, gardens, and land. If I did not use my own knowledge to effect this metamorphosis, it was not without regret, but I had to respect your scruples." Then, opening a little chest adroitly recessed into the wall, he said to me, "Here are the remains of that magical process," while at the same time showing me a box full of those gold pieces used in France. "As you know," he continued, "this is not what is least necessary to have when among us, and I thought myself obliged to keep a little provision for you."

I started to give him signs of my keen gratitude and of the admiration stirred in me by such thoughtful attentions, when Céline interrupted me and led me into a chamber next to that marvelous study.

"I wish to have you see the power of my art as well," she told me.

Before me were opened vast chests of drawers filled with wondrous fabrics, clothes, ornaments—indeed, with everything used by women and in such abundance that I could not keep myself from laughing out loud and asking Céline how many years she would have me live to take full advantage of so many beautiful things.

"As many as my brother and I," she replied.

"And my desire," I riposted, "would be that you both should live as long as I shall love you, in which case you will not die first."

As I finished saying those words, we returned to the temple of the Sun as they had named that marvelous study. Finally able to speak freely, I gave voice as I felt them to the sentiments that had penetrated me. What kindness! Nothing but virtue in the actions of brother and sister!

We spent the rest of the day savoring the delights of confidence and friendship. I hosted them for supper even more merrily than I had for lunch. I gave orders freely to domestics I knew to be mine, joked about my wealth and power, and generally did everything that depended on me to make my benefactors' good deeds pleasing to them.

As time passed, however, I thought I noticed that Déterville was lapsing back into his melancholy and that even Céline on occasion let slip a tear. Yet both of them recovered their air of serenity so quickly that I thought I must have been mistaken.

I made a concerted effort to convince them to enjoy with me for a few days the happiness they were providing me but did not succeed in this. We went back that night but promised one another to return shortly to my enchanted palace.

Oh my dearest Aza! How great will be my happiness when I can live in it with you!

XXXVI

Dearest Aza, the sadness of Déterville and his sister has only increased since our return from my enchanted palace. I hold them both too dear not to have hastened to ask them the reason, but seeing that they stubbornly persisted in keeping this from me, I no longer doubted that your voyage had met with some new misfortune, and soon my worry surpassed their sorrow. I did not hide its cause, and my friends did not allow it to last for long.

Déterville admitted that he had decided to conceal from me the day of your arrival so as to surprise me but that my worry was making him give up his plan. Indeed, he showed me a letter from the guide he had provided for you, and by calculating based on the time when and place where it was written, he gave me to understand that you could be here today, tomorrow, even at this very moment, but that in any event there were no more days to count before the one that would fulfill all my wishes.

After sharing that first secret with me, Déterville no longer hesitated to tell me the rest of the arrangements he had made, showing me the room he intends for you. You will stay here until, joined together, propriety permits us to live in my delightful chateau. Never again will I lose sight of you; nothing will keep us apart. Déterville has provided for everything and has convinced me more thoroughly than ever of the great extent of his generosity.

Now that light has been shed on this mystery, I am no longer seeking a cause for the sorrow consuming him other than your upcoming arrival. I pity him: I feel sympathy for his pain; I wish him a happiness that is in no way dependent on my sentiments and that will be a worthy reward for his virtue.

I even conceal some part of my elation so as not to exacerbate his distress. That is all I can do, but I am too preoccupied with my happiness to keep it entirely contained. Accordingly, much as I believe you to be quite near, much as I tremble at the slightest sound, much as I interrupt my letter at nearly every word to run to the window, I have not left off writing you, for my heart needs this easing of its elation. You are closer to me, it is true, but is your absence any less real than if the seas still separated us? I see no sign of you, you cannot hear me, so why should I cease conversing with you in the only way I can? Just another moment and I will see you, but that moment does not at all exist yet. Oh, is there any way I can make better use of what remains to me of your absence than in depicting for you the intensity of my tenderness? Alas, you have always seen it bemoaning its fate. How far that time is from me! With what elation will it be erased from my memory! Aza, dear Aza, how sweet that name is! Soon I will no longer call out to you in vain, you will hear me, will fly to my voice, and my heart's tenderest expressions will be the reward for your eagerness . . .

XXXVII

To the Chevalier Déterville
IN MALTA

Monsieur, were you able to foresee without remorse the mortal pain you were to attach to the happiness you were preparing for me? How could you have been so cruel as to have your departure preceded by such pleasant circumstances and pressing reasons for gratitude, unless it was to make me yet more sensitive to your despair and your absence? Brimming over two days ago with the sweetness of friendship, today I am experiencing on its account the bitterest of hardships.

Bereft as she is, Céline followed your orders only too well, giving me Aza with one hand and your cruel letter with the other. Just when all my wishes were being fulfilled, pain made itself felt in my soul. In recovering the object of my tenderness, I hardly forgot that I was losing the object of all my other sentiments. Oh Déterville, how inhumane your goodness is this time! But do not count on carrying your unjust resolutions through. No, the sea will not separate you forever from all that is dear to you. You will hear my name spoken, you will receive my letters, you will hear my prayers. Blood and friendship will recapture their rights to your heart, and you will return to a family to which I must answer for your loss.

What, as recompense for so many good deeds, I would poison your days and those of your sister! I would break up such a tender union! I would bring despair to your hearts even while still enjoying the effects of your acts of kindness! No, no, do not believe it. I see myself with nothing but horror in a house I have filled with mourning. I recognize your cares by the good treatment I am receiving from Céline at the very moment when I would forgive her hating me. But however great your thoughtful attentions, I renounce them, and I am leaving forever places that I cannot tolerate if you do not return to them. But how blind you are, Déterville! What error is it that brings you to a course of action so contrary to your designs? You wished to make me happy, you are only making me feel guilty. You wished to dry my tears, you make them flow, and in distancing yourself make fruitless your sacrifice.

Alas, you might have found all too much sweetness in that interview you thought so fearsome for you! That Aza, object of so much love, is no longer the same Aza I have painted for you in such tender hues. The coldness of his greeting, his praises for the Spaniards with which he interrupted a hundred times the sweet outpourings of my soul, the insulting indifference with which he plans to make only a brief stop in France, and the curiosity that is pulling him far away from me at this very moment all make me fear woes at which my heart shudders. Oh Déterville, perhaps you will not be the most unhappy for long!

If you are impervious to the pity of others, may the duties of friendship bring you back, for friendship is the only refuge for ill-fated love. If the woes that I fear were to befall me, what reproaches would you not have to make yourself? If you abandon me, where will I find hearts sensitive to my troubles? Will generosity, to this point the strongest of your passions, yield in the end to unsatisfied love? No, I cannot believe that, such weakness would be unworthy of you, you are not capable of giving yourself over to it. But come convince me of that if you love your honor and my peace of mind.

XXXVIII

To the Chevalier Déterville
IN MALTA

Were you not the most noble of creatures, Monsieur, I would be the most humiliated. If you did not have the most humane of souls, the most compassionate of hearts, would it be to you that I would make the confession of my shame and despair? But alas, what do I have left to fear? What is there for me to treat with care? All is lost for me.

No longer is it the loss of my freedom, my rank, or my homeland that I regret, no longer the anxieties of an innocent tenderness that wring tears from me; rather, it is good faith betrayed and love scorned that rend my soul. Aza is unfaithful!

Aza unfaithful! What power those terrible words have over my soul . . . my blood freezes . . . a flood of tears . . .

It was from the Spaniards that I first came to know misfortune, but the last of their blows is the most painful, for they are the ones who are taking Aza's heart from me: it is their cruel religion that authorizes the crime he is committing; it approves, indeed commands, infidelity, faithlessness, and ingratitude yet forbids the love of those closest to him. Were I a foreign woman unknown to him, Aza could love me, but because we are united by the bonds of blood, he must forsake me, must take my life from me without shame, regret, or remorse.

Alas, strange as this religion is, had it only been necessary to embrace it to regain that supreme good it is wresting from me, I would have subordinated my mind to its illusions. Moved by my soul's bitterness, I asked to be instructed in its ways, but my sobs were not heard. I cannot be admitted into such a pure society without giving up the motive inducing me to join it, that is to say, without renouncing my tenderness, an act tantamount to changing the nature of my existence.

I confess that this extreme strictness impresses me as much as it revolts me and that I cannot deny a kind of veneration for laws which, in all other matters, appear to me so wise and so pure. But is it in my power to adopt them? And were I to adopt them, what advantage would accrue to me? Aza does not love me anymore! Oh unhappy woman . . .

Of the simplicity of our manners, cruel Aza has retained only the respect for truth, of which he makes such dreadful use. Seduced by the charms of a young woman of Spain, ready to marry her, he agreed to come to France only to free himself from the oath of fidelity he had made me, to leave me with no possible doubt regarding his sentiments, to give me back a freedom I hate, to take my life.

Yes, it is in vain that he gives me back to myself, for my heart is his and will be until I die.

My life belongs to him. May he take it from me and love me . . .

You knew of my misfortune—why did you make it only partially clear to me? Why did you allow me to glimpse only suspicions that caused me to treat you unjustly? Ah, why am I accusing you of this as of a crime? I would not have believed you. Blind as I was, if warned I would merely have advanced my horrid fate, would have conducted its victim to my rival, and would now be . . . O gods, spare me that horrible image . . . !

Déterville, too generous friend! Am I worthy of being heard? Forget my unjust behavior and pity an unhappy woman whose esteem for you is still greater than her weakness for an ingrate.

XXXIX

To the Chevalier Déterville
IN MALTA

Since you complain of my behavior, Monsieur, you must be unaware of the state from which Céline's cruel attentions have just drawn me. How could I have written you? I thought no more. Had I retained any feelings, surely confidence in you would have been one, but surrounded by the shadows of death, the blood frozen in my veins, I was long unaware of even my own existence and had forgotten everything down to my misfortune. Oh Gods, why in bringing me back to life did you bring that dreadful memory back to me as well!

He has left! I shall see him no more! He flees me, he does not love me anymore, and he has told me so. Everything is finished for me. He is taking another wife, he is abandoning me, for honor condemns him to do so. Well, cruel Aza, since Europe's bizarre code of honor holds such charms for you, why did you not imitate the artifices that accompany it?

Fortunate women of France, you are betrayed but long enjoy an illusion that would now be my sole possession. Dissimulation prepares you for the mortal blow that is killing me. O dreadful sincerity of my nation, can you really cease to be a virtue? Courage and forthrightness—are you crimes when the occasion warrants?

You saw me at your feet, barbarous Aza, you saw them bathed in my tears, and your flight . . . Terrible moment, why does your memory not tear my life from me?

Had my body not succumbed to the throes of pain, Aza would not be triumphing over my weakness . . . You would not have left alone, Aza, for I would be following you, ingrate, I would see you, and at least I would die before your eyes.

Déterville, what fatal weakness separated you from me? You would have come to my aid. What the disorder of my desperation could not accomplish, your reason, capable of such feats of persuasion, would have obtained. Perhaps Aza would still be here. But having already reached Spain with all his wishes fulfilled . . . Pointless regrets! Fruitless despair . . . ! Pain, oppress me.

Monsieur, do not try to overcome the obstacles keeping you in Malta to return, for what would you do here? Flee an unhappy woman who no longer feels the kindness she receives, who makes a torture of it for herself, who wishes only to die.

XL

[To the Chevalier Déterville]

Rest assured, overly generous friend: I did not want to write you until my days were out of danger and, less distressed, I could calm your fears. I live; fate wishes it so, and I submit to its laws.

The attentions of your kind sister restored me to health, and some return of my reason has sustained it. The certainty that my misfortune is without remedy did the rest. I know that Aza has reached Spain and that his crime has been consummated. My pain has not disappeared, but its cause is no longer worthy of my regret, which, if any remains in my heart, is due only to the suffering I have caused you, to my errors, and to the derangement of my mind.

Alas, as that reason enlightens me, I discover its impotence. What can it do for a despairing soul? Excessive pain gives us back the weakness of early childhood. As then, only concrete objects can affect us, and it seems that sight alone of our senses has access to the most intimate recesses of our soul. I have cruel experience of this fact.

As I emerged from the lengthy and oppressive lethargy into which Aza's departure plunged me, the first desire inspired in me by nature was to retire to the solitude I owe to your foresight and kindness. It was not without difficulty that I obtained from Céline permission to have myself driven there, where I find aid and comfort in warding off despair that social life and even friendship would never have provided me. In your sister's house, her consoling words could not outweigh those objects that were forever retracing Aza's faithlessness for me.

The door through which Céline conducted him into my room the day you left and he arrived, the chair on which he sat, the place from which he told me of my misfortune and returned my letters, down to his shadow erased from a panel where I saw it form all caused new sores to open on my heart each day.

Here I see nothing that does not remind me of the pleasant notions it caused me to entertain at first sight, and I find in it nothing but the image of your kindness and that of your charming sister's.

If Aza's memory comes to my mind, I see it from the same perspective I saw it then and believe myself to be in that place awaiting his arrival. I give myself over to this illusion so long as it is agreeable to me. If it leaves me, I turn to books. Reading at first with effort, I find that imperceptibly new ideas form around the horrid truth buried at the bottom of my heart and in the end offer some respite from my sorrow.

Shall I admit it? Freedom's great sweetness enters my imagination at times, and I listen to it attentively. Surrounded by pleasant objects, I strive to savor the charms of their orderliness. I am in good faith with myself and count little on my reason. I give myself over to my weaknesses and combat those of my heart only by yielding to those of my mind. Maladies of the soul do not suffer violent remedies.

Perhaps your nation's lavish notions of decency do not allow a person of my age the independence and solitude in which I now live, or at least so Céline tries to persuade me every time she comes to see me. But she has yet to offer strong enough reasons to convince me. True decency is in my heart. I render homage not in any way to a simulacrum of virtue but to virtue itself, and I will always take it for my actions' judge and guide. I dedicate my life to it, and my heart to friendship. Alas, when shall it reign there uncontested and uninterrupted?

XLI

To the Chevalier Déterville
IN PARIS

I have received at practically the same time, Monsieur, news of your departure from Malta and of your arrival in Paris. Whatever pleasure I may feel at the idea of seeing you again cannot overcome the sorrow caused by the note you wrote me on arriving.

Oh Déterville! After having taken it upon yourself to conceal your sentiments in all your letters, after having given me reason to hope that I would no longer have to combat a passion that grieves me, you abandon yourself more than ever to its violence!

What is the use of affecting a deference that you contradict at the same moment? You ask permission to see me, you assure me of your blind submission to my wishes, and yet you endeavor to convince me of the sincerity of sentiments that could not be more opposed to those wishes and that offend me, wishes of which I will never approve in any event.

But since you are seduced by a false hope and abuse my trust and my state of mind, I must tell you of the resolutions I have adopted, resolutions more steadfast than yours.

It is in vain that you would flatter yourself to think that you can make my heart take on new chains. The betrayal of my trust does not undo my oaths. Please heaven it should make me forget that ingrate! But if I do, I will remain true to myself and not be unfaithful to my own feelings. Cruel Aza has abandoned a possession that was once dear to him, but his rights over me are no less sacred for having done so. I may recover from my passion, but I will never have passion for anyone but him. All the sentiments that friendship inspires are yours, and you will never share them with anyone else, for I owe them to you. I pledge them to you and will be faithful to that promise. You will enjoy my trust and sincerity to the same degree, which is to say that you will enjoy both without limit. All manner of vivid, delicate feelings that love has produced in my heart will turn to the advantage of friendship. I will allow you to see with equal frankness my regret at not being born in France and my insuperable penchant for Aza, the desire I would have to owe you the advantage of being able to think and my eternal gratitude to the person who obtained it for me. We shall read from each other's souls. Trust is as capable of making time pass quickly as love. There are a thousand ways of making friendship interesting and of driving boredom from it.

You will give me some acquaintance with your sciences and your arts; you will savor the pleasure of superiority.

I will regain the upper hand by developing virtues in your heart with which you are not acquainted. You will adorn my mind with that which can make it amusing and will take pleasure from your work; I will endeavor to make agreeable to you the childlike charms of simple friendship and will find happiness in succeeding at this.

By sharing her tenderness with us, Céline will infuse our conversations with the merriment they might otherwise lack. What more will be left for us to desire?

You fear needlessly that solitude might damage my health. Believe me, Déterville, solitude never becomes dangerous save on account of idleness. Always occupied, I will know how to fashion new pleasures from all that habit renders insipid.

Without gaining deeper understanding of nature's secrets, is not the mere examination of nature's marvels enough to bring constant variety and renewal to ever pleasant occupations? Does one lifetime suffice to gain a superficial yet interesting acquaintance with the universe, my surroundings, my own existence?

The pleasure of being—a forgotten pleasure not even known to so many blind humans—that thought so sweet, that happiness so pure, "I am, I live, I exist," could bring happiness all by itself if one remembered it, if one enjoyed it, if one treasured it as befits its worth.

Come, Déterville, come learn from me to economize the resources of our souls and the benefits of nature.

Renounce tumultuous feelings, those imperceptible destroyers of our being. Come learn to know pleasures innocent and lasting, come enjoy them with me.

You will find in my heart, in my friendship, in my feelings, all that can compensate you for the ravages of love.